S·T·O·R·I·E·S
IN ANOTHER
L·A·N·G·U·A·G·E

Yannick Murphy

S·T·O·R·I·E·S
IN ANOTHER
L·A·N·G·U·A·G·E

ALFRED · A. · KNOPF

NEW · YORK · 1987

THIS IS A BORZOI BOOK
PUBLISHED BY ALFRED A. KNOPF, INC.

Some stories in this work were originally published in the
following publications: *The Malahat Review*, *The Quarterly*,
Southwest Review, and *StoryQuarterly*.

Grateful acknowledgment is made to *The Antioch Review* for
permission to reprint "Mercury" by Yannick Murphy, which
first appeared in *The Antioch Review*, Vol. 44, No. 1, Winter
1986. Copyright © 1986 by The Antioch Review, Inc.
Reprinted by permission of the Editors.

Library of Congress Cataloging-in-Publication Data

Murphy, Yannick.
Stories in another language.

I. Title.
PS3563.U7635S7 1987   813'.54   86-46012
ISBN 0-394-55707-7

Manufactured in the United States of America
FIRST EDITION

TO MOM AND DAD,
AND TO RAY, MICHELE, AND JOËLLE,
AND TO GORDON

The author thanks the editors of *The Antioch Review*, *The Malahat Review*, *Southwest Review*, *StoryQuarterly*, and *The Quarterly* for permission to reprint some of the entries herein. The author also wishes to acknowledge her gratitude to Kate Walbert.

The Escape   3

The Slit   9

Red, Red   19

The Summer the Men Landed on the Moon   27

Ball and Socket   39

Believer in Death   49

The Headdress   57

The Toys   67

Mercury   75

Laws of Nature   85

Rough Seas   93

Tidal Air   99

Where Dead Is Best   109

Contents

The Children Inside the Trunk   117

Stories in Another Language   125

A Good Father   135

The Killer   141

S·T·O·R·I·E·S
IN ANOTHER
L·A·N·G·U·A·G·E

THE
E·S·C·A·P·E

They left Mukden in the morning. The mother told her daughter to keep track of the days and the nights. Because on the train, she said, the windows would be boarded up and there would be no way to tell.

The mother owned a pair of black shoes with rhinestones on the buckles and rhinestones on the heels, and when the mother and the daughter went to bed, a light from the corridor came in under the door of their room and made the rhinestones on the buckles and on the heels shine. The daughter told her mother that she thought the rhinestones looked like stars.

From Mukden to Paris it would take one month to travel by train. The mother said to her daughter that those were the only two places she would have to know, Mukden and Paris, because whatever is in between those two places, she said, are places you will never see.

At night, before the mother went down the corridor and into the bathroom, she would say to her daughter to watch out for her shoes so that no one would take them. After the mother left the room, the daughter got out of bed and tried on her mother's shoes. When the mother came back and saw her daughter wearing the shoes, the mother said to the daughter, "Thief, thief, and half my size!"

The boy in the next car was the daughter's age. He had small toy metal trucks and when the daughter first saw him, he was shaving his mother's head with a toy metal truck. When the boy gave her one of his toy metal trucks to play with, the daughter went to her mother and made the toy metal truck climb her mother's shoulder and go onto her mother's head, and the daughter said, "Mama, I am going to shave your head now."

The mother laughed and said that it was all right.

The daughter made the noise *shrr, shrr* and said, "Your hair is falling to the floor."

When the mother and the daughter walked to the dining car, the mother always walked in front of the daughter and wore the rhinestone shoes. The daughter said to her mother, "Under your feet you've got matchsticks, or something, because sparks fly from the floor when you walk."

When it was time to sleep, they could not sleep. The mother said to her daughter, "I will make you a bet. I will bet you that all the people who are sleeping now are wrong, that it is really daytime and not nighttime, and that we cannot sleep because we are the only ones who know what time of day it really is out there." Then the mother pointed to the boarded-up windows of the train.

Because they could not sleep, the mother and the daughter talked about things to do that they could not do on the train. They talked about ice-skating, and the mother got out of bed and put on her slippers and showed her daughter how to skate backwards.

The daughter did not skate backwards so well in her own slippers, so then her mother let the daughter put on the rhinestone shoes and they turned off the light and the mother said to the daughter, "Ice-skating backwards will come easy to you if you just watch where the light from the rhinestones is going and not the backs of your heels."

When the daughter saw the boy from the next car, she asked him if he knew where diamonds came from. But the boy said that he did not want to talk about diamonds. He said, "My mother says she is bald. She says she has no more hair left for me to shave off. I am going back to Mukden," the boy said. "I hate this train."

"Diamonds," her mother said, "come from penguins' tears." Then the mother said, "No, don't listen to me, diamonds are like wood. They are hard."

Then the mother said to the daughter, "Here, wear these for the rest of the ride and sleep with them on to keep them safe from thieves."

The mother woke up screaming.

She ran to the windows and banged her fists against the boards.

"I have been here before!" the mother screamed. "Open the windows and let me see! I have been here before, and we are passing too quickly. Let me see!" she screamed.

Then the mother said to the daughter, "Give me a shoe," and the daughter gave the mother a shoe and the mother used the shoe like a hammer to bang on the boards that covered the window—and out of the buckles and out of the heels the diamonds flew loose and everywhere and in the dark like shooting stars.

THE
S·L·I·T

H er mother was fat and she was fat and when her mother threw herself down into the grave, on top of her daughter's box, what I thought was that she was doing the Fat Man Dance with her daughter, and then I remembered that not every family did the Fat Man Dance.

It was the same with pogo. It was not until I went to school and got sick and lay on the floor in the bathroom, and the girls came up around me, and what they told me was that they could see my belly button.

I had never heard of belly button. It had always been pogo.

I thought, what is belly button? I thought, what kind of a name is that for my pogo? I wanted to go home and I wanted to ask someone at home who started it that we had pogos, and why was it that all the other people had belly buttons.

I thought, I bet the daughter's glad she's dead, because what her mother was doing, throwing herself into the grave on top of the box like that, looked funny. It looked funny because her mother was fat, and it looked so much like the mother was doing the Fat Man Dance, because her arms were spread out too, as if she were waiting for her daughter to spread out her arms also, and then they could hold hands and smack bellies together and dance in circles on the box just the way we always did in the summer when we did the Fat Man Dance. Because we always did the Fat Man Dance in the summer when we ran around with no clothes on and danced a lot because it was summer.

Then I realized that there were no flowers in the place. I looked around, at the other headstones, and there were no flowers. I thought to myself that this must be the wrong place to bury the daughter, that her mother had made a mistake, because if the mother wanted to do the Fat Man Dance with the daughter, she would have also probably brought flowers to put on the daughter's headstone. I thought to myself that my mother would not have buried me here. I do not know where my mother might have buried me, but maybe she would have done it out back, in our backyard. Maybe my mother would have buried me under our pool, in our backyard, and then in the summer she could swim over me, her belly facing down.

The daughter's father told us a story.

He told us that when the daughter was little she went home from school, at lunch, and after she ate lunch she started playing with her dolls, and she forgot about the time, and she didn't know what to do—if she should go back to school and have her teacher get mad at her, or if she should just stay at home and keep playing with her dolls—so what she did was she wrote a note, and she went back to school, and what the note said was *Dear Teacher, please excuse Jody for being late—she had to feed her dolls.*

I heard someone call it a VJ. But we had always been calling it a free-free. Maybe this was because my sister and I used to always look at the back of cereal boxes where there was a toy inside the box, and what the back of the box said was *FREE-FREE, Inside This Box Is A Toy*, and I think my sister and I would think to ourselves it was a free-free inside the box.

The last thing I did with Jody, I think, was play Foot.

We were on a bunk bed, on the top bunk bed, and we were just talking—and then we started kicking at each other, and then we started playing Foot.

I never understood Foot. It was something you did just to see how long you could push your foot up against the other person's foot, or see who could push the other person off first off the bunk bed. It was something like that. Maybe it wasn't really the last thing that I did with Jody, maybe it was just the last time that I touched her.

There was a drop of blood on the ground. When I think about it, I still don't know why I did not think there was something wrong. It looked like something our dog would leave behind on the floor when she was in heat, and we could know where the dog was going across the house that way, and my mother would say, "Oh, the dog is in heat," when she saw the blood, and it was all right because we knew it, so no one was supposed to get upset about it or worry. I don't even think we even cleaned the drop of blood up from the dog. I think we just left the drop of blood on the floor in the house.

There were also people standing in their doorways. But everyone does that. But later I should have thought to myself that it was not summer and that people only stand in their doorways for no reason like that if it is summer.

When I got upstairs, there was no answer at her door. Then I saw that the neighbor's door was open and I heard Jody's mother inside the neighbor's place.

Her mother wasn't saying anything that I could understand. She just sounded like she was laughing. Jody and I were supposed to go out that night and I wanted to know if Jody was going to come out. But her mother was laughing and it was hard to understand what was going on. Then I saw her mother and I saw that she was crying, not laughing, and then she came over to me and gave me a hug. But to me it felt more like a hang. She just let all of her body hang down on my back and I thought my legs were going to give. She was crying into my hair and I thought about how I had just washed my hair because Jody and I were going to go out that night.

"Where is Jody?" I said.

Her mother could not say. But the neighbor said, and then I left.

Going down the stairs, I touched my hair—and it was wet where her mother had cried against it, but the even more amazing thing was the blood I saw in the street when I looked down. I saw that there were more drops of blood than I had thought there were before, and they were all over, spread out, as if our dog, in heat, had run in circles on the ground.

I saw the people still standing in their doorways. I thought that maybe they thought that if they stayed out there long enough, that it would happen again, or that Jody would come back and open the door to her place.

Then I thought her mother pushed her.

Sometimes I have dreams where someone is trying to show me a picture of the way Jody looked on the ground, or sometimes she comes back and I think to myself that I can't wait to wake up and tell everybody that Jody is back. Sometimes I tell Jody that she should have stayed around. Sometimes she shows me a bed with the sheet pulled back and the window open. Sometimes she makes hairbrushes and bottles and things move in the room by just looking at them in my dreams.

Maybe the last time I touched Jody was in the bathroom when I was passing her a napkin under the stall door—and when she took the napkin from my hand, she touched my hand at the same time.

Her father pulled out a rose from inside his jacket. I did not understand how her father could have kept it there so long and how it still was in good shape and the petals were not bent.

My father gave us the names of mushrooms. My sisters were Faerierings and Moonlights, and I was an Inkycap.

My mother gave us butterfly kisses on our cheeks.

When her mother threw herself onto her daughter's box, I thought that maybe she did not throw herself onto the box right, that maybe she threw herself only half onto the box, and where her face was on the box was where Jody's free-free was instead, and what Jody's mother was doing was giving Jody's free-free one of those butterfly kisses that my mother used to give to us.

Her window was the kind that is low to the floor and when you stood next to it, it hit you in the place in your legs that made you feel as though it would be so easy to fall out of it.

We used to rub butter onto our pogos.

Really, we rubbed it all over.

It felt good.

We would hold the stick of butter in its wrapper just the way you would if you were buttering a pan for a cake, and we would move the stick of butter around and in circles.

You could tell that her father wanted to throw the rose on top of the box, but that he could not because her mother was still on top of the box. Then he got down next to the box, and he pulled on her mother's arm.

Once we got pencils and put them in our free-frees so that they hung down, and we said that we were cows. Other times we played Superman, and put towels between our cheeks in our bottoms and ran down a hill and yelled, "Superman!" and hoped that the towels would lift up into the air, like a cape would do, if we were wearing capes and running down a hill.

Before they put her into the box, they told us they dressed her in her St. Claire's Confirmation dress. She had already grown out of that dress and I didn't know how they could have fit her into it. I pictured a slit in the back of her dress that they made so that the dress would look like it fit Jody from the front.

Then I thought, maybe, for some reason, they don't put them in faceup, but they put them in facedown, and that if the top of the box was taken away we would see the slit in the back of her dress.

I thought, if the top of the box was taken away, then Jody's mother's face would be in the slit on the back of Jody's dress if they had put Jody in facedown.

I saw her father pull on her mother's arm a little more. Her mother put her arms around the box like she was hugging the box and she would not move. The rose he was holding started to bend where his hand was around it.

Lately, I have been dreaming that she is standing over me in my bed. When I wake up, I do not let myself open my eyes. I think, maybe now that the dress is very, very small for her, she is a doll wearing a dress. Then sometimes I think that when I wake up that I can smell her, or that I can smell dirt, but then the wind comes through my window and I can't smell the smell.

Now I hear them saying U*ra*nus instead of *U*ranus, the way it always used to be said.

My father wrote our mushroom names on a wall in our house, but we don't live in that house anymore.

When her father was getting her mother to get off the box, and when her mother was standing up, after he had pulled her up, her father slipped and his leg hit the box and it made him fall down onto the box, and what he was doing was sitting on top of the box, with the rose still in his hand, and what it looked like he was doing was that he was asking her mother to marry him all over again, as if her father was sitting on a log in the woods and she was just standing there, listening to him, and we, all the mourners, were the trees.

I guess if my mother could, if people allowed it, she would bury me under her bed, so that when she was sleeping, she could sleep belly-down.

Then he put the rose on top of the box, and we all walked away and heard them shoveling the dirt on top of the box.

I thought about the rose being on top of Jody's belly and about the dirt being on top of Jody's belly, and I thought about Jody doing the Fat Man Dance down there even after her mother walked away.

RED,
R·E·D

Today the river is going up. I have told her about it but she tells me that all things start from the mountains and then go down. I tell her this river is going up. She tells me my father will come down from the mountains and she tells me to watch for him.

I cannot pray enough so I pray all of the time. I do not see my father's face any longer but I see what he must see, he sees the river going up, and away from Saigon.

Also, everything is now going up her face. The sunlight goes up her face because her head is leaning back and I can see inside her. I want to call the nurse. I want the nurse to let down the sides of my mother's bed and walk my mother through the halls, showing the others what my mother looks like inside.

"Ten men rode by that window and did not take their hats off when they saw me," she says.

I tell her the men wore no hats. I tell her they were tied by their hands and came down from the hills like goats or like sheep and not like men.

"Tell me what they said," she says, thinking maybe that they know where my father is.

Smoke from her mouth goes up and into her nose because where they put her, by the window, is cold.

The men give me francs, rolled very thin, that they carried up inside of them when they walked over the mountains. I wash the francs out in a basin and my sister says red, red, and swirls her finger in the water that turns red from the blood that was on the francs.

I have looked at the K's keys for a long time now, and they are not keys anymore, they are things that if only I was strong enough I could lift with my thoughts and open the gates for the men.

My sister thinks that my father will come home because every night she sees him lifting his feet up and down.

One man says that the river is not the same today. He is a man with no chin. I thought to myself his words did not mean anything because his words must have fallen so quickly from his face and down onto the ground. The K asks me what he says and I tell the K that the man is looking for food.

Today my sister wants to wear my rope-soled shoes. I don't let her wear them and she walks barefoot behind me, and people are looking at us because my sister is yelling at me to give her my shoes. I stop and I take off my shoes and I give them to her and then I start to pull her dress off. I tell her I want to wear her dress. After I pull the dress up over her head, I almost think she will not be my sister anymore but somebody else, maybe one of the men from the hills.

I leave her there standing there naked, except for my rope-soled shoes, then she walks behind me, quiet, waiting, I think, for me to throw down her dress that I have not put on, because I cannot possibly wear it because it is much too small.

When I go in to see my mother, I am still holding my

sister's dress and my mother does not say that she knows what it is, but when my mother sees the dress, she takes it up to her neck and wraps it like a scarf, saying that it is cold where they put her and that her fingers have all become one on each hand and are as useless as the flippers on turtles.

I want to turn my mother upside down and let my sister's dress fall from her neck and be on the floor so that my mother will see that it is my sister's dress and that I have left my sister outside where it is cold, standing in just rope-soled shoes that are too big for her because they are mine.

The man with no chin tells me to take hold of my own hand and then he takes hold of my hand and he says, "See, holding on to your own hand is not like someone else holding on to your hand." His hand is like my father's hand. His fingers are long and become thin toward the ends like the ends of candles become thin.

When I go down to the river, I see the pilings where piers used to be and the pilings stand up in the water, at a slant, like they were trying to go up but a wind pushed them over and almost back down flat into the water.

Now I am giving the man with no chin a plate of food when the K is not looking because I think that if he has something under his chin to catch his words, I can see what he says.

He says he has seen my father.

"Under the bed I have a sweater," my mother says.

I go under the bed and there is nothing. I look under the slats of the bed and I pull out straw and I show it to her. She brings it to herself and says that it smells like outside, and she says she is better now, knowing that she is lying on what is outside.

My sister says she is seeing his arms as well as his legs.

One man gives me francs and when I wash them in the basin, there is a kernel of corn and my sister takes it, saying she will grow a stalk behind the gates where the man is.

She cannot see the river but she says I am right, the river is going up and not coming down from the mountains. I tell her what about my father. I tell her my sister has seen his arms now. I tell her I pray so much that my prayers are on top of each other and it is not hard to do anymore but is something to do, like lifting my hands or holding my hands. She says it is my father pulling up the water from the river and carrying it over his back like a sack up and down hills.

My mother's bed is not by the window. She is up farther now, her head to the wall. She says my father carried her there.

My sister is outside. She is leaning against the wall and a K is taking her picture. He is asking her to put her hands on her breasts but also asking her to move her fingers apart, so that he can see her buttons between her fingers.

The K calls them buttons.

My sister puts her foot out and I can hear her asking the K if he can get in a shot of her rope-soled shoes.

The men call them Toulouses. They are always asking to see my Toulouses. I have a friend who has bigger Toulouses than I have and I bring her in sometimes and I show them hers. They pay me in francs. While she is showing them, I can see some of the men going back behind a corner, bending over, and pulling the francs out. Sometimes one man will help another man pull them out.

They call each other Monsieur Banker.

I am Mademoiselle Bouche.

The man with no chin calls me Maman sometimes, saying he feels like the child inside the woman, with the woman being the one to speak for both. "Tell them I am one of you," he is always saying to me.

My sister is keeping things up inside her now. She has learned that she can keep my mother's diamond ring there. She has gone out on mornings just to walk through the slums with the diamond ring up inside her.

She says that when my father comes back she will be able to fit the gold up in there and maybe even a watch.

She drinks only water.

She takes small steps.

The man with no chin went today. I watched him. His head hit the wall hard like it was as scared as his back was when his back went against the wall the first time he came here. I looked at his chin the whole time. I told myself that if blood came down it then my father was dead, and I told myself that if the blood did not go down it, then my father was alive.

I did not get to see where the blood went. A K came over to him and was putting his hands in the man's pockets.

Every day now my mother is saying that it is getting colder, but it is getting warmer. She says with this cold the water in the river will freeze and the water will not go up or down.

I sit down and watch the hills when I think men are coming down them. But I see when they come closer that they are goats or sheep. A man is with the goats or sheep, pushing them with a stick.

THE
S·U·M·M·E·R
THE MEN
LANDED
ON
THE
M·O·O·N

Down at the reservoir Ray Petes was showing us how he chopped wood in half with his hands. He said we could do it also. He said that all we had to remember was to keep our eyes on the middle of the wood before we hit the wood with our hands.

We liked watching him chop the wood. But we never wanted to chop it ourselves. Chopping it just looked too hard to do and it looked like it would hurt our hands. We were down at the reservoir because we were waiting for night to fall. We had to wait for night to fall before going swimming in the reservoir because we did not want to get caught and we did not want someone to come by and tell us to get out of the reservoir and to tell us to stop swimming there.

Some nights we took one of the old rowboats with the holes in it from on shore and we took it out onto the middle of the reservoir and drifted around in the rowboat until the water came through the holes and made the rowboat go down. We sank so many rowboats in the reservoir.

Back on shore, in the house, we always thought about the water we were drinking and if, in the water, we could taste paint chips from the sides of the old rowboats we had sunk or if we could taste the T-shirt Suzy Petes had thrown off herself one night and declared it was a skinny-dip night. After that, every night was a skinny-dip night, and we just left our clothes on the shore and did not let them fall to the bottom of the reservoir.

We thought Ray Petes chopped wood in half like that—I mean so much of it and toward nightfall—because he was thinking about his dead son.

His son was named Michael.

When we were in an old rowboat, and drifting around, we had to fight our minds hard and try not to sing the song about Michael rowing his boat ashore because we did not want Ray Petes to hear us singing that song when he walked back up the hill to his house after chopping wood in half with his hands.

That summer we stayed in a cottage.

The cottage had gun holes through the walls because, we thought, kids in the winter walked around in the woods, out behind in the back of the cottage, and shot at animals they could not hit. So then the kids shot at the walls of the cottage because they must have felt they had to hit something.

It was the summer the men landed on the moon.

Ray Petes lost Michael on horseback. Ray Petes was riding one of his horses and he had Michael sitting in front of him and they were riding along and a dog came by and spooked the horse and threw the riders, Ray Petes and his son. Ray Petes fell one way and Michael fell the other way, his head hitting a tree.

The dog was still alive. The horse was not. We saw the dog sometimes and threw stones at it.

. . .

Ray Petes never went swimming with us. He always went back up the hill, to his wife, who was in the house, who we thought was putting the others to bed.

On the other side of the reservoir, on the side of it that looked the same as the side we came in from but wasn't, and the side that felt different and darker, we could see the house sometimes and we could see Ray Petes standing in the window looking out somewhere. Some of us thought he was looking down at the other side of the hill, to his mother's house, and thinking about if she was all right. Then some of us thought he was looking down at the pond where we caught crayfish and that he was thinking about nothing or that he was thinking about Michael.

We never stayed too near the other side of the reservoir for very long. We wondered out loud if some dark night we would ever get confused and walk onto the shore, on the other side of the reservoir, thinking that it was our side of the reservoir, and walk up to a house that looked like our house but wasn't.

We each had a gun hole that we called our own. Some of our holes looked out onto grass or onto a tree. Some of our holes looked out onto mushrooms. But I think the important thing was what passed by your hole as you were looking out of it. Seeing a raccoon got you someone else's dessert after dinner, seeing a squirrel or a bird got you only half his dessert. Someone saw Ray Petes through his hole and we had to give him all of the desserts we had gotten that week because seeing Ray Petes outside one of those holes, in the back of the woods, was a thing we all hoped to see.

We played gin rummy on a big glass table. We also learned how to cook and we all learned how to boil frankfurters. The

Peteses' kids had us over for dinner and they made us boiled frankfurters. Then we had the Peteses' kids over for dinner and we made them boiled frankfurters. We told each other how the boiled frankfurters tasted different depending on the plates that you used to put them out on. We all decided flowered plates made boiled frankfurters taste better, or I think that's what we all decided.

Ray Petes was always doing things with wood. He made a chair in the shape of a swan that fit two and rocked like a rocker, but really three could play in it because one had to be conductor and tell us all the places we were going to see as we rocked. Because that was the summer other people had already done it, we were going to see the moon.

There was a spring at the top of the hill, before the path, that led down to the reservoir. The spring, we thought, had the best water in the world. We never seemed to go to the spring, we always seemed to come across it, and when we came across it we always remembered how good it was and we would get down beside it and all of us would drink from it. We touched cheeks as we drank from it and we laughed at ourselves because we thought we looked like horses drinking from the spring instead.

We found out which tree it was. Even though it was so long ago, we still found a place in the tree that we thought was made from Michael's head or even from Michael's teeth, that we thought might have hit the tree first even before his head. But then someone said it probably wasn't Michael's teeth and what the place probably was was from Ray Petes trying to chop down the tree with his hand. It was too long ago to think that there was still blood on the tree—but we looked for it, anyway.

You could not help but think what fish swam beneath you when you swam in the reservoir. So during the day we decided we would catch all the fish so that we could swim without thinking about the fish in the reservoir at night.

We only caught sunnies.

We learned how to cook them and we floured them and fried them in butter and called their tails dessert because we ate their tails last.

One night Ray Petes took us out in his boat and took us night fishing. We caught pickerel and eels and no sunnies. We could not stand the sight of the pickerel and the way the eels wound up the line of the fishing rod like they were not being caught but like they were catching us instead. We dove off the boat and into the reservoir and stayed swimming in the water for a long time and we told each other we felt safe in the water because already our old rowboats were sunk at the bottom and Suzy Petes' T-shirt was down there also.

As we swam, we heard Ray Petes in the boat. We heard him bang a coffee can of worms against the side of the boat, and we heard him move a life jacket across the floor of the boat, and we heard him sit on the bench of the boat after having been standing, and then someone whispered, in the dark, that the bench Ray Petes was sitting on he could probably chop in half with his hand.

We all knew he could do that anyway—but doing it out in the middle of the reservoir was something we had never seen him do, and we wondered if Ray Petes really would ever think to do that himself. A crack like that in the night, over this calm water, someone said, could raise the dead.

There was a tree that had branches like rungs on a ladder and we climbed the tree sometimes just to see what was going on in every direction that we could see in. Once we saw Ray

Petes down by the graveyard walking through the rows made by the headstones that stood side by side. Other times we just saw birds in the sky and animals on the ground.

Their land was Headless Horseman land.

You did not forget it when you were walking back up the hill at night after swimming in the reservoir. When you were walking up the hill, you were trying not to think about it, but when you looked at someone else you knew they were thinking about it, and we always ended up by running up the hill, on back up to the house.

They said, in order to be safe from the Headless Horseroad. We tried, every night, to remember to put our pennies there, on the stone wall—but sometimes we forgot. When we forgot, Ray Petes was always the one who gave us pennies and walked with us onto the road, late at night, to put the pennies he gave us down on the stone.

Ray Petes built the dock when the skunk cabbage was flowering, so no one went down there to watch him chop up the wood because no one could stand the smell of the skunk cabbage those few days it flowered.

When we finally went back down to the reservoir, the dock was finished and the skunk cabbage smell was gone. It was a windy day. Ray Petes' rowboat was tied up alongside the dock and it was already beginning to hit against one of the poles from the dock every time that the waves from the reservoir came under the rowboat, and what we could already see was beginning to happen was that the pole, being hit by the rowboat in one place over and over again, was getting a place cut into it that looked so deep we thought we were going to see blood coming out of the wood.

One day we got tired of the gun holes in the walls of our

cottage so we took tape and taped over the holes. Then it was daytime but it felt like nighttime with all the holes in the walls of the cottage taped over.

We went and sat in the swan, and our conductor told us that what we were passing through was a jungle with snakes that hung down from the vines of the trees, and we decided that that wasn't what we wanted to see and we asked to get back on the trip that went to the moon.

One night there was no moon and the sky was darker than we ever remembered before.

Swimming in the reservoir, we swam close together because we were afraid we would lose each other. That night the water felt like something else than water, it was not cold and it was not hot and if it were not for the fact that we could lift the water up in our hands and hear it splash back down onto itself, we did not think we would have been able to tell that we were swimming in water at all.

We became lost and we could not find either side of the reservoir to swim back to. After a while, we decided we would swim toward the middle of the reservoir, and we decided that if we just kept our eyes on what we thought was the middle we would find our way back to the shore.

The next thing Ray Petes started to build was a raft for us that we could hide in the bushes during the day and bring out into the water at night.

It took a long time for him to finish building the raft.

When we saw the dog that spooked the horse that threw Ray Petes and Michael, we threw sticks for the dog to fetch in the road, in the middle of the road, and we hoped for cars to come by and kill the dog.

Ray Petes left his tools down by the reservoir at night, under a woodpile, and we went there one night and took the ax from under the woodpile and walked back up the hill. But this time, though, we were not afraid of the Headless Horseman because we had the ax in our hands, and then we thought we found the tree in the dark that Michael was thrown against and we set the ax in the place in the tree and pulled back up with the ax and then hit it against the place again, hoping to cut down the tree.

We tried for a long time, but we could not cut the tree down. All we did was make the place in the tree look deeper and new again.

After Ray Petes saw the tree he said since we thought we were so good with his tools that we could finish the raft he was building ourselves because, he said, he wasn't going to.

When we got to the raft, in the dark, we thought he was kidding, we thought the raft looked finished already, and we launched it, thinking we could swim all night in the reservoir and use the raft to come back to and to lie on when we became tired of swimming, and just stare at the sky.

When we got to the middle of the reservoir, the raft sank. We tried to hold it up, but we couldn't. After a while we just swam away from it.

The next day we were up in the tree that had branches that looked like rungs on a ladder and we could see Ray Petes finishing chopping down the tree that we had started to chop down the night before, and what one of us swears he saw was that the last chop Ray Petes took at the tree, before the tree fell, was a chop with his hand.

Nights after that that we swam in the reservoir we never got lost again. Not even on the darkest, most moonless nights.

We didn't know why. We thought maybe it was because we could always find the middle of the reservoir again if we had to, knowing that it was right where the sunken raft Ray Petes built for us was. After that, we thought that the drinking water tasted different also. Not only did we think that the water tasted like the paint chips from the sides of the old rowboats with the holes in them, and that it tasted like Suzy Petes' T-shirt, but that it tasted, we thought, like the raft and like Ray Petes' hands where he had touched the wood of the raft when he had built it.

BALL
AND
S·O·C·K·E·T

At first I thought it was safe to dance with my father, that he would not push his leg between mine, but then I realized it was dangerous and that I would show him anything, I would show him how my breasts shook as I danced and I would look to see if he was watching mine or somebody else's.

He said turning left or right was always a sure thing when I sat on the handlebars; fifty pounds made it hard to make a false move. You are my Buddha, he said, my small kid fitting in between my arms whose belly I can reach up and touch at every red light.

I saw him cry from joy when he hugged my brother at my brother's wedding. Then my brother cried also. But I knew it was false and not a sure thing, no one cries from joy, a person cries because he is losing someone, or because he did not spend enough time with someone.

In cold weather, the mist I breathed out he swallowed in his mouth and said something like that would keep him going till noon.

Bad luck, he said, felt like when his small Buddha got down from the handlebars, to him lightness never felt good.

At home, he let me stand on his feet and we walked to the kitchen and back, he said he could teach me to dance that way. I told him the box step was easy, I could have learned it on my own two feet, not standing on his. He taught me how to play the piano, but that was hard, when he pulled his fingers out from under mine, I could not follow his rhythm.

One day he said I had grown too big for the bicycle. My feet touched the ground and he said turning left or right was a chore. I told him the bigger the Buddha, the better the luck. He laughed, he said he did not deserve all my luck and that he wanted to ride alone. In a way, he said, I want to get hit, and I fear for your life, or my life in taking yours. If we stopped short he would let one hand go and use it to hold back my chest. I thought his hand stayed there a while, even after we had been safe for some time.

I would lift up my shirt and show him the places on my back that itched so he would scratch them, and when I was sick I told him the only thing that helped my belly was to lie across his.

When I rode with him all I saw were my feet near the fast-turning spokes and the sides of his arms, hairy with spots that I thought the smell of him came out of.

When fishing, he planted me before him and showed me how to cast. He said we will catch Buddhafish who sit at the bottom, but I did not think of the Buddhafish, I thought of how my shoulder fit neatly between his legs as we swung back the rod. It was a ball and socket motion that made the line fly.

He told me his mother taught him to fall asleep with his arms crossed over his chest so if he died in his sleep he would be ready for the coffin.

I rode our big dog like he was a horse, my father bent

down close to my ear, he said what he would not give to be little again, a baby Buddha holding on to the scruff of the neck of our dog.

I watched him watch other women's breasts all the time.

I grew long hair, I asked him to brush it, he said cut it short. He was the one who cut my hair. I heard him say to my mother, I know the shape of her head better than you do, this kid's head is flat in the back, he said, you hang a picture there, it will lie like it's on the wall. When he did my bangs, he pulled my head back toward his belly and said it did not feel like a head, he said it felt like the palm of my hand was there.

When he pushed his leg in between mine I moved back. He said I should have stayed there, though, he said he was falling and then he asked if that is what I wanted, for him to fall down at his only son's wedding.

I showed my father that my brother looked at me when I danced. I showed my father that the bride looked too, she looked at my breasts. She watched my brother watch me wanting to be watched by my father, who was looking at another woman, maybe my brother's bride. Then nothing was safe. Maybe his leg in between mine was safe, for a moment, before he fell to the floor. His leg let me think about how old he was and that putting his leg in between mine was as far as his body would go.

He lost the hair on top of his head when he was sixteen. He said all that is passed on through the mother but I cannot believe it, not when I can see the scabs on his bald head from hitting low doorways. He is the living proof, after all.

I brushed the hair that was left over, the hair on the sides of his head. I used the soft brush that was made for a man.

It had no handle, it was meant to fit in the palm of your hand. He said he could not feel it go through his hair, he asked me to use my fingers instead.

He rode me in the rain. Those days he used one rain poncho to cover us both. He wore the part over his head that you can see out of, but I rode in the dark. I heard him tell people on the street, who asked him, that I was his Siamese twin. In the dark, I held onto the handlebars with tight fists, I thought I would lose my balance because all that I could smell was him under the poncho.

Riding in the rain, it was cold. His warmth held the smell. It stayed on my back and my neck after I had gotten off the bicycle. I took his smell to school every day that it rained and I was afraid that my teacher would think I was wearing my father's shirt, and only the poor kids wore their fathers' shirts.

Because I could not see what he said to people I imagined he frowned a lot. I did not hear people laugh when he told them I was his Siamese twin. They must have seen pain in his face. Because they could not see me, I thought then neither could he. I thought, if his bald head had hair, I would not blame him for passing on baldness. What you can see always makes for a sure thing.

When we flew birdy he put his feet up high on my chest, saying my belly he dare not harm, round perfection he hated to push out oblong. He had my baby nipples between his toes. Facing him was hard, he pushed, with his feet, his heaviness into me. I could not breathe. I was flying in the room. He made me touch my nose to the bedside table and my toes to the sheets. I had thought heaviness could only come down, it came up though, from him, and I was scared, I did not want my ribs to meet my backbone. I did not want him to have to reach inside me and pull them apart.

My knees smelled of pavement. It was an iron smell, like

blood. It was a hard smell, my knees hurt. My father helped me up off the curb. He looked at me as if wanting to know why I fell off the handlebars, didn't I know that good luck Buddhas had to be strong? They did not fall down for no reason. I had a reason, I was looking up. I had never looked up the entire ride to school before. I had been fighting not to look at the spots on his arms. I thought looking up would be good, who would dare make a little girl fall off the handlebars of a bicycle while looking up at the sky at the same time? It was my pose of looking heavenward that I thought would save me. It did not save me, I thought, because at the time I was not thinking of God, I was thinking of how to make my father stop riding me to school so that we could turn back for home. I had just learned to drink tea. I wanted to go home and drink tea with him. I wanted to make the tea for him. He knew about cavemen. I thought he could tell me again about life in a cave and life without fire.

We did turn around, he told someone we did not know on the street that it was not a day for school, not when his Buddha fell from the handlebars, when just at rest, waiting for a light to change. He said he would not be caught dead without me if that is how the day began.

At home, he drew a caveman scene on my palm for me. The feeling of his pen drawing on my palm shot through to my belly button, then down to where it made me want to pee. I wondered if that was the way to learn, not to hold the pen with him, but to let him draw on me. Later on in the day, I tested it out, I tried to draw, but my skill was not any better than it was before. I wore out the drawing on my palm by stamping my hand against the bathroom walls but the image was reversed, and because it was false and not the real thing, I did not feel guilty about signing my name to it.

Then he danced with the bride. He cut in on her dance

with her father, he walked up to her, he must have thought this is what he waited his whole life, as a father, to be able to do at his son's wedding. He crossed lines that were complicated. The bride and her father looked alike. Her father must have looked at my father's face, hoping to find that my father did not look like his daughter, my brother's bride. Then her father looked over at me, he must have seen that I do not look like my father, maybe he also thought that he looked a little like me, to get back at my father. I thought to myself, I do not want to dance with that man also. People would get confused, they would want to know who the father of the bride was. I had to tell them. I cut in on the bride and my father, I thought to myself, I am doing this woman a favor, this man puts his leg between yours and everyone will think he is your father.

As my teeth grew in, he put his finger in my mouth to feel them. He checked the baby teeth for looseness. He showed me how to check them myself, then both of our fingers were in my mouth at the same time. My saliva on his finger he did not wipe on his shirt or his pants, instead he used his hand to smooth down my hair.

He told me to let the dog lick my cuts, he thought what was in dog's saliva had a natural cure. One day, I did not tell my father, but I let the dog lick a cloth, then I went to my father and patted the scabs on his bald head with the cloth while he slept with his arms crossed.

Some nights I went to his bedside and thought about uncrossing his arms for him, I thought that if I uncrossed them, he would never die, because he would never be ready for the coffin. I did not do it, because in his sleep his arms looked heavier and if I touched them I might find that he was already dead and I was keeping his body from going to heaven.

He said he did not wish for me to be as light as a rabbit's foot and that it was good I liked being picked up all the time.

Before the bicycle, he carried me on his shoulders, and asked me to look out for low doorways. He told people, one of the reasons he had me was so that he could carry me on his shoulders and so that I would put my hands on his bald head as he walked.

Then, at the wedding, I thought he wants to marry me. Maybe, I thought, he thinks that it would be like marrying the half of him that is a girl, or the half of his life that he did not live, or the half that takes the leg between hers and knows what it's like for the other half also.

The day I grew too big for his shoulders was a winter day. I blamed it on the hat that he wore. I was jealous that it was on his head, closer than my hands could be and better than I could cover his baldness. Then I blamed it on the cold and that was useless. The cold came every year, it was not something he chose or wished for to happen, except, maybe, in the heat of summer when he told me that although there was no breeze, me standing in the doorway made him hotter.

He also said that I made the fish go away. He said they've got ears and that they hear me humming when I'm sitting on the rock while he demonstrates casting. He said me standing in front of him and the two of us casting together did not work, that we both had too much swing and that the trees took advantage of our strength and caught our lines like they were the hungry fish on dry land.

After he cried, he turned to me at the wedding. I thought I saw him wanting me to be little again, fifty pounds of good luck to prop on his shoulders and walk through the guests; holding onto my thin ankles where his hands would make two warm spots against my skin.

Then he smiled, to him it was simple and not dangerous, a father and a daughter courting until death made them part, a pact in the night to leave his arms crossed was the only vow, silently, that I ever made. He made no vows to me. If he could, maybe he would have promised to keep me little his whole life, a good luck Buddha whose belly he reached up and touched at every red light.

BELIEVER
IN
D·E·A·T·H

Fourth of July we went over to Claris Jones' roof and hardly saw what was going on at the river. At the river they had the big fireworks coming out of the tall ships, but on Claris Jones' roof we had sparklers that came out of cardboard boxes my mother and Claris Jones had bought when they had gone down South in Claris Jones' car.

When they talked about their trip down South, they talked about it like they had been gone for years, but they had only been gone for a week. Sometimes Claris Jones would say what she would not give for a cup of Stuckey's road-stop coffee or a pecan log, right now, at that very minute. She also said that picking the sparklers to buy was not an easy thing to do. She said that there were so many colors of sparklers to pick from down South that she began to think that up North we did not have the same colors at all.

I had only been with my mother and Claris Jones in Claris Jones' car when we had gone to the dump. They liked the dump. They sang songs as we drove down the streets to get to the dump, like it was a long trip they were going on and not just a ride through town.

I ran up to them once, when they were holding ice-cream cones in their hands after they had gone to the dump alone, and I was hot and the ice-cream cones were just what I wanted, but when I got up close, and Claris Jones put the ice-cream cones in my hand, I saw that they were plastic ice-cream cones and not real ones.

I also saw that Claris Jones had dirt on her chin.

Claris Jones laughed and I watched the dirt on her chin spread wide like it was a second smile she had drawn on herself. My mother laughed also.

You could get things like that at the dump.

We found plastic frying pans with plastic strips of bacon and plastic eggs in them. Claris Jones said she wanted everything and then she took it all back to her house, up to her roof.

She called her roof the upstairs room. She said being outdoors all the time reminded her of being down South. She had car seats on the roof and mannequins to sit in the car seats, and pies of plastic pizza that the mannequins looked like they were ready to eat. Claris Jones said, when we were all up on her roof, that she didn't think of us like ourselves, and that she thought of us like we were the mannequins. She had a love seat on the roof that she had made out of two tires and Claris Jones called it the Underdog. She said I looked as if I should have been part of the love seat when it was first made, and that she was sorry I wasn't around when she first made it. Then she asked me if I wouldn't mind coming over to her house sometime and sitting in the Underdog all day.

On the water, Fourth of July was all right, but the fireworks in the sky, coming out of the tall ships, was just like noise you would hear on the street out your window at night, and we didn't really seem to hear or to watch. Claris Jones was writing my name in the sky with a sparkler. I was still young and I could not read backwards so well, so Claris Jones had to tell me what she was writing. I still don't think I can read backwards so well.

Anyway, Claris Jones' dog, Benno, did what he always did when he was bored, or so Claris Jones said, and Benno ran down to her room, went to her dresser, and brought up the keys to her car. But I saw that Claris Jones wasn't ready to notice him yet. She said, sometimes when he does that, that if she waits long enough, she can get two tricks out of him instead of one. So she waited a while and wrote my mother's name in the sky, but because my mother's name is long you had to remember the first part of the name while the last part was still being spelled out, on account of the letters were always fading so fast in the dark. Then Benno played dead and, before I knew it, we were all walking down Claris Jones' flights of stairs that never seemed to end and made you think to yourself that you never thought, in all your life, that walking down stairs and not up them could make your legs hurt so much.

But Claris Jones had a good way of making the walk seem shorter. She pointed to the landings we walked across and said here, here is where I found my cat, Vito, and here, here at the next landing is where Vito died. Then, at the last landing, Claris Jones said here, here is where I want to die.

Outside, it seemed like the seconds took turns being daytime and nighttime because over the river the fireworks were still lighting up in the sky. So when we got in the car it was nighttime, and the trees on Claris Jones' block, even though it was July, had no leaves or branches on them and so, in the dark, as the car pulled away, it looked like we were passing through poles that lined the sides of the block and not passing through trees. One hand on the steering wheel, Claris Jones used the other one to salute the trees on either side of the car, then she put her head out the window and shouted, "Next time you see me come through here, let's have a twenty-one gunner out of you!"

My mother—a believer in death, she called herself—said out the window, on her own side of the car, "And make that one for me, too!"

That night, it being the Fourth of July, everyone was at one end of the river, watching the fireworks, and not at the other end of the river where the dump was. Driving under the highways, Claris Jones and my mother kept wondering out loud about the things they might find at the dump that night. My mother said she knew she'd find it if she just looked hard enough for it, she wanted a lamp with the base made in the shape of a boat. Claris Jones decided she didn't care what she found, and that even if it was a plank from the pier by the side of the dump, she'd take that back to her upstairs room.

Driving in the car, with the windows wide open, we smelled the river and we smelled the pickles being made in their barrels in the warehouses on the waterfront. Then my mother and Claris Jones broke into song and sang "Swing Low, Sweet Chariot" and "Over the Rainbow."

When we got close to the dump, Claris Jones and my mother stopped singing, as if, I thought, it was a sacred burial ground that they were coming to and did not want to speak near or in it. Claris Jones drove the car slower, so that riding on the cobblestones made me think that it felt like a journey in a covered wagon and not like a drive in the car. Then, for some reason that I did not know at the time, Claris Jones stopped the car.

Everything was quiet until Claris Jones said slowly, in a whisper, "Mecca, it's just like Mecca." My mother said, "Ah, yes—when will it ever end?"

I saw them gazing out in front of them at something I could not see.

At first I thought the street was moving. At first it looked to me as if the cobblestones were small waves lifting themselves out of their holes in the ground and going back down into their holes again.

You didn't want to just start up the car again and drive through rats like that. Rats like that traveled in a pack so big that you couldn't tell where the pack began and where the pack ended. You couldn't even tell, at first, what direction the rats were moving, there were so many of them. It was something you had to sit and wait out and at the same time watch because, really, you could not believe what you were seeing.

I saw Claris Jones and my mother and I heard them roll up the windows, then say Hail Marys.

I did not know what Hail Marys were. But I started saying what Claris Jones and my mother were saying.

The rats kept moving, kept crossing. You could spot your eye on one of them and follow it moving to the other side, but then sometimes your eye would lose the rat, and you would look at another rat and you would tell yourself that you are not going to lose this rat this time, but you do, you always lose your eye on the rat you picked because there are just too many rats and this was not something you were used to seeing, so many rats crossing a street all at once.

I go back to that side of town sometimes and I can't find the dump. My mother tells me it's still there. My mother says on

Claris Jones' grave she would swear to it that dump is still there, even if the smokestacks at the site of the dump and the pickle warehouses can't be found.

We live in a tall building now. I go up to the roof and I can see for miles. But I still can't see the dump. Fourth of July, we go up to our roof and watch the fireworks coming off the river. But we don't write our names in the sky with sparklers anymore. My mother says that she thinks that because Claris Jones is gone, that the rats are gone also and my mother says she still wonders if down South is still down there too, and she thinks that maybe everything is all up here now, up North.

THE
H·E·A·D·D·R·E·S·S

U p at the falls one night he put her head back with his hand and then he put a sword down her throat. The others remember that night, as well as that day, because that was the day that the water below the trestle had flooded over and they could go swimming in it. That day both of them held hands and did lovers' leaps from up top of the trestle and down into the water.

I wasn't supposed to see what the Bucks and the Does were doing. I was not a Buck or a Doe. But that day I walked down the path behind the Bucks and the Does and their leaders. Their leaders were Touché and Karen. Touché was Head Buck and Karen was Indian Doe. I never knew why they didn't just call her Head Doe, like Head Buck was called, or why they didn't call Head Buck Indian Buck, like Indian Doe was called, but I was not a Buck or a Doe and I would never understand, they said, until I did become a Buck or a Doe.

That morning, before I went down the path behind the Bucks and the Does, I looked out across the road at a house that was on the other side of the road. I felt bad for the house because it was not on our side of the road and because it was not like the rec room or the lower field tom-tom house, where we would all get together at night, before bed, and the Bucks and the Does would sit us on their laps while Touché and Karen told us about Wild Man and how Wild Man lived up by Sunset Rock.

Then I didn't feel bad for the house anymore because then I realized that the house never had to hear the story about Wild Man who lived up by Sunset Rock and that the people who lived in the house never had to hear the story about Wild Man who lived up by Sunset Rock and that the people who lived in the house probably slept at night.

I didn't sleep at night.

At least it never felt like I slept at night, or when I did sleep at night, I remember I dreamt that my brother was Wild Man up by Sunset Rock. My brother had been a Buck there years before. My brother had come back after one summer, and he said, at home, to my mother, that he was Head Buck, and my mother said there were no Head Bucks in her house and that there was only her and him and me. But for the longest time, my brother said that he was Head Buck.

So my mother said that my brother had turned into a wild boy at that place.

It had been raining ever since the last Run Amok Night, but we wore shorts, anyway. The Bucks and the Does told everyone that if we all wore shorts that we could make the sun come out.

The rain hit our legs.

I looked out across the road, at the house that was on the other side of the road, and I decided I wanted to go to the other side of the road, so what I did was I walked down the path behind the Bucks and the Does who were going out past the gate, and I remember I looked down at the grass that I was stepping on, and I remember I was thinking that it was grass that only Bucks and Does ever stepped on and that, I thought, my brother, being Head Buck, must have stepped on first, the first summer when he was Head Buck and had gone out first past the gate. I wondered then who was his Indian Doe.

Touché and Karen turned around while they were going and they told the other Bucks and the Does that the first stop was the trestle. I stayed back and I hid behind trees and I don't think that then the Bucks and the Does ever saw me.

At the trestle, they all walked over the rotting wood of the trestle like it was nothing, like it was just the plank of wood that was over the ditch in back of the lower field tom-tom house that we walked across every night.

I could see that Karen and Touché were the first to take off their shirts and their shorts on top of the trestle. Touché had hair in his eyes and it was dripping with rain and the rain was falling down into his face from his hair. Karen's hair between her legs was dripping with rain also, and the hair there hung down straight, and it looked like one of the arrowheads that were on the walls of the rec room, arrowheads found by Bucks and Does on overnights up by Sunset Rock.

I thought, with the water coming down from what looked like her arrowhead between her legs, that what Karen looked like she was doing was peeing, and it looked like a pee that would never stop because the rain looked like it would never stop.

I saw Touché take Karen's hand and I saw that Touché and Karen were almost the same color from the sun and I remember I wondered if that was why they were Head Buck and Indian Doe.

As they jumped, Touché and Karen were still holding hands, and when they came up for air, out of the water, they raised their hands held together up into the air as if, I thought, to show the other Bucks and Does whose hands it was that had never come apart under water.

After my brother had come back, he was darker from the sun also, and he wore a towel around him after taking a bath, and he walked around the house with the towel around him, and I remember I could see where his skin was white, where the towel did not cover his white skin, and I remember my mother asked him to at least cover the white skin up, because she said walking around like that, with his white skin showing, looked like he was walking around with nothing on at all.

Then the Bucks and the Does got down into the water, below the trestle, where the water below the trestle was shallow, and they all held hands and stood in a line from one side of the trestle water to the other side of the trestle water, and they walked over rocks. From where I was, it looked to me as if the Bucks and the Does were coming at me, like they were a plow on a farm going through a field and clearing the field.

But the deep water stopped them from coming at me.

When they came to the deep water, their heads went down below the water and then, when they all came up for air, they all lifted their hands that they still held together, up into the air, and they yelled.

I did not hear what they yelled.

After my brother came back that summer and he was still thinking he was Head Buck, he asked me to sit on top of him. He was lying on his bed and he held me while I sat on him and he moved me up and down on top of him and he kept his eyes closed and his mouth open. After some more of this, my brother called me his Indian Doe.

. . .

Touché and Karen told the other Bucks and the Does that the second stop was the falls. I had heard that the road up to the falls was a winding road, and I had heard that it was hard to go up it, but that once you got up to the top of it, it was not like down below.

When the Bucks and the Does went up the winding road, they still held hands, and they never looked behind them, and it looked to me as if the Bucks and Does were plowing the road.

At the top of the road, I could not see the Bucks and the Does at every turn, and the only way that I knew that they were in front of me was because they were singing as they were going. I can't remember what they were singing. It was a song I had never heard. It was a song, I thought, that they made up to sing while they were going up the winding road together because they were Bucks and Does and because no one down below could hear them sing.

Up at the top of the falls, I wondered if we were near Sunset Rock.

I remembered Wild Man lived up by Sunset Rock.

It was still raining, and the Does would wring out their hair as if they did it all the time, as if wringing out their hair was the same to them as putting their hair behind their ears, and the Bucks shook the hair on their heads dry, and then I saw them scratch themselves where it was wet between their legs.

After my brother had been back for a while, he gave me a feather for every time that I sat on him. He said, "Keep it up and you will have a headdress."

My mother saw my feathers, and she said that they were

pretty and she said my brother must be changing his ways and not being the wild boy anymore.

Then I heard Touché telling the Bucks and the Does that they were going to spend the night at Sunset Rock, above the falls, and that anyone who didn't come along wasn't going to be a Buck or a Doe anymore and would probably be taken by Wild Man on their way back down the winding road because Wild Man got Bucks and Does who went alone.

It was the night that Touché found the sword on Sunset Rock. And it was the night that he put the sword down Karen's throat while me and the Bucks and the Does watched. Touché said it was Wild Man's sword. He said Wild Man had left the sword up on Sunset Rock for us to use.

First Touché took the sword and brought it up over his shoulder and then he hit the rock hard with the sword and the sword made such a loud noise that I thought that probably the others could hear it also. I mean those who slept in their beds back down at the bottom of the falls.

Before Touché put the sword down Karen's throat, he told her not to move. He told her that he had learned this from someone who had told him that it was something that people had to do together. He told her that both of them had to do it right or it would not work. Touché put Karen's head back with his hand and then he put the sword down Karen's throat. It looked to me like Karen was quiet, but I saw her eyes blink, maybe because the rain was falling into them.

While the sword was down in Karen's throat, I heard Touché say, "Indian Doe."

Then I heard the other Bucks and Does sitting around Sunset Rock say, "Indian Doe."

I heard myself say it, too.

· · ·

My mother remembers that summer after my brother came back as the summer that he was the wild boy. Now she says she is glad that he is not that way anymore.

I still remember how the Bucks and the Does held hands and jumped off from up on the top of the trestle and how they still held hands while they came up for air, and I still remember watching Touché put the sword down Karen's throat—and I still think that that is what Bucks and Does still do.

THE
T·O·Y·S

MIE is not hearing. She is that way sometimes, but then when you think her mind is off to a place that is nowhere near where you've been, she says something. After he told the story of him walking down the dirt road with no shoes on, she said, after a long time, "Were you a nigger when you were a boy?" and he did not say anything to her. He said to me, "What is there to say?" and I thought to myself that he is probably wishing she falls back into not hearing again.

I want to know about the books. I want to know how he carried his books when he walked down the dirt road. But he does not say. I think maybe he is thinking that he really was a nigger when he was a boy because he had no shoes. I think maybe he carried his books with an old rein from a horse and that the leather was cracked. I ask him if that's right, if that's how he carried his books. He says, "Yes, that's how I did it." But I think he is not hearing me anymore. MIE can do that, she makes everybody sit around and not hear like her sometimes.

MIE is particular about what she sits on. Often I have to

run and get her a throw for the chair before she sits down on it. He says get her a throw from the wash pile, but I don't do it. I know she will know if it's a throw from the wash pile. I ask her why she can't just sit on the chair without a throw, and she says she is afraid of the bugs coming up from the ticking in the seat. I picture the palm trees on the road and I think how you never know that there are rats living in them until the rats move and then they make the sound of the dry sound that someone makes when walking through cornstalks in a cornfield.

He says she is not coming to church. He says she will sit in the house all day because that is what she wants to do. I ask her why she is not coming, but MIE is not hearing at the moment. I wonder if she would come to mine. But there is no way to tell if she would.

Pa is taking my hand and walking me down the road to the church. I look down at Pa's shoes. They have lines in the leather like the lines around a person's eyes.

The church is cool inside and I think of the maple out back by our house that we all sit under on a hot day. MIE does not sit on the grass under the maple like the rest of us, she sits on a throw on a chair we bring out from inside the house. MIE does not ever sit in the sun, so under the shade of the maple is the only place she has ever sat out back by our house.

Dr. Crowley is coming up to Pa and holding Pa's hand like Pa was Dr. Crowley's girl and Dr. Crowley is holding on to Pa's hand so long, thinking maybe that all of what he wants to say to Pa will come out best through his hand and that he has to hold on to Pa's hand for a good long time because he has got a lot to say.

Throughout it all at church I am thinking about Pa walking down the dirt road without any shoes on. It fills all of what

I can see up and I am not seeing the preacher giving the sermon, I am seeing the road ahead of Pa and Pa's dusty feet and Pa feeling the books in his hand and holding on to them by cracked old horses' reins. I am seeing Pa being a nigger, then Pa not being a nigger, and changing that way while he's walking under trees and then walking out from under trees.

First thing I tell MIE when we get back is that it was like sitting under the maple. She wants to know if we could see Lonnie's face. I try to remember Lonnie's face, but all I can see is Pa's face being Nigger and then being Pa's face again, and I can't remember if they laid the top open.

That night the others are riding their toys in circles on the road. It is late, but I go out and join them. We ride in little to bigger circles. We do it for a long time. I am thinking that that is all I am meant to do, go in circles around a smaller circle and have a bigger circle going around me. It is the wheel in front of me that I look at all the while. If I look at it all of the while, I can begin to think that it is not just taking me in a circle but that it is taking me to places, places which not even MIE has been to.

She met Lonnie on a boat and that is where they married, on the boat. She said she threw her flowers into the ocean afterwards, because she had no girls around to catch them. She says she gave the right to mermaids to love mermen because of the flowers she threw. I can picture the mermaids, but I cannot picture the mermen. I always thought that mermen were fish and nothing else but fish. But she says they are half-fish like any other mermaid is half-fish.

I picture Lonnie with the top open and all of a sudden I remember what I was seeing at the church and I am not seeing Pa's picture inside me walking down the dirt road anymore. I think maybe that is the way the not hearing is also.

She is answering everybody's questions. "I did not go,"

she answers, "because I did not want to see him looking like he has never looked before. I did not want to see mine looking like that," she says.

I tell her it was nothing different. I tell her it was like she had asked him what the first thing he ever remembered was and he was trying to think backwards, and the thinking backwards was better if he was lying down still with his eyes closed.

She has eyes where the black is not all black and the white is not all white and it looks like the black has run onto the white or the white has run onto the black, making a cloud in her eye, or maybe the black and the white were having a war with each other for space on her eye, so that her eyes, in the end, would be either all black or all white. Under her eyes, it looks like Dr. Crowley came with a needle and pulled out all the color there and left the black.

Her face is a berry. It is round. I think she is a berry that can grow in the shade. I think she is a blackberry. I think blackberries grow in the shade. I think she is maybe a blackberry fallen down to the ground already. She has always said heat rises. She is a cool blackberry lying under a bush she has fallen off.

"Mine, mine," she keeps saying and holding the pillow to herself.

I think she is holding it because it is a cool pillow, but Pa says it is for warmth, for a kind of cold she has in her that she cannot warm. I know the pillow is cool. I have put my head on a cool pillow at night even when the night was hot. Pa is trying to take the pillow from her but it is like all of herself is in her hands right now, and there is nothing left inside of her and all of her that is able to hold the pillow is in her hands because the rest of her is nothing and she is in her hands.

Pa says she will leave soon. But she is not leaving. Every day she sits with a pillow against her. Pa tells her that if he were a rich man, he would if he could. MIE does not answer. She has begun not to eat. I see Pa asking her to take the corn he took off the cob with his knife and buttered and mashed himself. He lifts the fork to her mouth. She is not hearing now and she is not answering and she is not eating.

Pa says he can do it no longer and he gives me the fork to give her the corn with, but she won't take it from me, either. I think maybe if I put the fork to her hand, her hand would open up like a mouth and take the corn.

Dr. Crowley comes to visit with her to find out why she won't take the corn. He looks into her eyes and asks her please to take the corn, but I think that today the white has won in her eyes and there is no black left in her eyes to see him with. I want to tell Dr. Crowley about the war in her eyes, but he sits me down and tells me that I must put the food on her lips so that the taste of the food gets on them and makes her open her mouth.

I have not told Pa but now I lay food on her pillow so that she will take it. This morning I lay a spoonful of applesauce there, and she bent over the pillow and ate it, not even using her hands. It looked to me like she was kissing the pillow.

Pa says he would not do it if he were not a poor man. Pa says, though, that it was not written in the stars, that he had walked his mile with no shoes and that was the mile he would walk for the rest of his life.

Pa's feet are in me again. Like the night I followed the wheel in front of me and it took me to places that were far away, Pa's feet walking down the road are inside me and making me not hear or see the way MIE does not hear or see.

Later, it comes back to me what Pa said.

He said MIE would leave tomorrow, that he would take her to a place he knew and that if my mother was around, she would take her to that place, too.

Pa tries to take the pillow from her, but MIE screams "Nigger!" at him, and he pulls away from her like he thought when she looked at him that he really was a nigger, and then Pa looked to me like he needed to get to a mirror fast, to look at himself and see if it was true.

Pa is still trying to get MIE out of her room. But I have seen that no matter how thin an old woman is, you cannot move her when she is in her hands and is holding herself tight.

M·E·R·C·U·R·Y

A sking if anyone knew where Mercury was, my mother meant the dry cleaners.

Undoing her bra, she showed us a magic trick so old, and pulled it through the sleeve of her shirt.

When my mother passes by where the cat was put in the ground, she says I want to be burned, I would rather you sift through my bones with your fingers than remember the dirt. Someone always places a rose on top of the cat, we remind her.

I wear black, she says take it off, you are too young.

Ask her how she will pay for it next, with what? Your good looks? She says no, I've already used all that up.

We can remember the cigarettes she has smoked. It goes like this—Chesterfield, Pall Mall, Tareyton. She says they sound like stops on a train.

This is her standing poolside, her toe pulling up water, a drain so deep she dives down for it.

Thanksgiving she tried to run over a pheasant. It was something she wanted to put on the table. I remember going back and forth in the car, stopping and going, and her missing each time. At night, she said, listen up, I hear the pheasant in the woods.

At the movie, ask her what happens next, and she will tell you. She is always right.

I like it when she dances, she bites her bottom lip.

Belly up, she said, your plane will land belly up. Stick to the rear, learn to smoke, she said, my children.

I can do the trick now too. But it was better watching. When she took it off they looked like they were still in there, pushing out on all sides.

She's got these legs that never quit. She calls them her eighteen hours. But we know she's had them her whole life.

When she comes back, and she is hot and wet, I try to imagine what she looked like before she was fat. But that was a long time ago. There are pictures—lumber jacket, string bikini. I remember her putting wax on her legs, while she stirred soup in the pot.

When the hurricane hit, she made us stay up and watch the skylight glass ripple. Don't sleep, she said, knowing that you could die any moment. So we stayed awake, no one was ready to die for a moment.

I am half Chinese, she said, from Northern China, where our fathers' noses were long.

When she could not find the cleaners, we all told her it was a far way to go, and very high up. Just one skirt, she said, is that so much to ask for? She looked up Mercury in the phone book, we told her it was like looking up under "S" for the Sun.

These are words she cannot say—crustacean, Neanderthal, Woolworth's, responsibility, nasturtium, Abominable Snowman. This is what they sound like when she says them—Croatian, Nanderthal, Werewolf's, ressponsibility,

Nastersheeum, Abomenablah Snowman. There are others but those are the ones I remember. We have Croatians in our yard. Sometimes she calls the kitchen the chicken.

She's got this thing for the back of my neck. It reminds her of me as a baby. She would pick the one thing I cannot see in the mirror. Besides, it feels as old as my hands and my arms and my face and my feet. I have looked at my sister's neck. If you watch it long enough, it begins to look as important as a nose or a belly.

We drove to the next town, where they sold grain alcohol for canning. But she made us stop by the roadside and lift the dirt from the farmland in our hands. She said it was black dirt and called it the richest. It was like that in China, too, she said.

Someone brought her a bottle filled with her homeland. I saw her pour it out onto newspaper and search for small twigs.

When she found Mercury, no one believed her. She showed us the skirt and said it was clean living proof. No one believed they had skirts on Mercury.

Later on, she said she had really been searching for stones, not twigs, and that it was something I had made up in my head.

Then someone says my sister looks like the Mona Lisa, and my mother says, no, she's prettier than that. So I look at my sister again. When she smiles the pink above her teeth shows and is wet. I look at the family pictures and none of the long-nosed Chinese men, or women, have mouths like that.

When we threw all the old furniture into the street, we sat down in it afterwards and rested. Outside, it was not our furniture. Once it is out, it belongs to the street, my mother said. So sitting in the chair, she did not cross her legs or crack her bad toe. On the street, we talked about the lives of the chairs. This one has no arms, she said, and it was the one your sister sat in. This one was yours, I can tell, each year you would add another pillow to keep the bottom from falling through.

Sometimes you can catch her placing a rose on top of the cat.

Then she said there really was no Mercury cleaners, just the usual place that uses safety pins to keep her skirt on the hanger and the words on the tissue that read "We do quality work."

So when driving in the car, we stopped telling her to watch out for rabbits or potatoes that had fallen off big rattling trucks.

I sat down with her and looked through the pictures of all the long-nosed Chinese men in our family, whose names were all either Fouz or Pouz. I told her she looked like they did and I knew she did not believe me, because no one had told her so before. Really, she looked like the women, who never smiled in front of the camera because it brought on bad luck.

Remember, she said, the Chinese nursery rhyme about the frog on the lily pad? No one said anything, it was never forgotten.

Next Thanksgiving, we had turkey. She tilted the pan in the oven and brought up the juices with a spoon.

We stopped telling her that Werewolf's was Woolworth's. We let her look at the back of our necks.

She told us that when you iron, you do the sleeves last, so that is what we did, and we waited for her to tell us to stop, and tell us to do the most wrinkled parts first, or however we wanted. She said I was born with a caul on my head, and that meant good luck. She said fire with fire, two birds with one stone, starve a fever, spilt milk, ashes to ashes, a gift horse in the mouth, coming up roses, itchy palms, red sky at night, step on a crack, needle in your eye, wing and a prayer, spit and glue, as high as the moon, over the rainbow, a rolling stone, cold hands, warm heart, straight face, people who live in glass houses, where there's smoke, a watched pot.

We wanted to see the trick, but she had started taking it off in the bathroom. When we walked in there, it was strung over a pipe.

So when my sister and I could not take it anymore, we walked to Mercury. We were hoping to find a pheasant along the way. Our mother stood at the door and waved a stick. You can't teach an old dog, she yelled.

On the street, we sat on a couch and thought about the people the couch belonged to. We were jealous of them for not having a mother like ours. We slid our hands behind the cushions, looking for clues to prove that we were not the only ones.

Next day, the ocean was like a lake, and there were no waves. Swimmers floated, my mother, a swimmer, lay on her back, closing one eye, to keep out everything, including the sun. We waited for her to say hotter than hell, when she said it we walked back up to the sand, put our hands on our knees, and started waiting it out.

If I asked her what it looked like, I think she would say it was covered with lily pads, not cities with carts or countrysides with rice paddies.

> *Eegah hamah, suh tiao twei,*
> *Liang jih yen ching,*
> *Eechung tsuei,*
> *Pilah-Palah, shiah liao shwei.*

> *A frog, four legs,*
> *Two eyes, one mouth,*
> *Pilah-Palah, jumped into the water.*

One day she looked down and said the street made meat-eaters out of birds. Pigeons ate leftovers. Sparrows waited around for them to finish.

It was not easy, waiting it out. There was no place to do it. Stand at the top of her backyard and you would feel like you would tumble down past the rose bush.

Falling star season, we lay on the trampoline. In the dark, we could feel the moves she made bounce back up to us. We rocked that way every time she pointed to the sky.

She pulled out a sweater that had wax drippings on it from candles we used during the blackout. Wear it, she said, you will catch cold if you don't.

Now they are flying into planes, buzzards and birds of prey are killing pilots, she said.

The rabbit, we told her, is not like the finch who flew into the window, the rabbit is there in the road, if you kill it, it is no accident.

We wanted to put Mercury back in her head.

My brother had liquid mercury in a jar. He would turn it over to watch it break apart and then go back together again. He also made toy soldiers, then melted them down to make more.

She gave me ten dollars and said go buy the best god-damned thing. I came back with a magic trick set. She looked at the bag and quietly said, Werewolf's, no, Woolworth's.

So I showed her a few tricks, and she used the black hat for her jewelry, saying the felt kept it shiny and safe. Then I cried and she showed me where a mouse had run up her leg. Thinking it was the cat's tail batting against her, she did not scream.

My mother can't be called Ma, because if you do, she won't answer. She says it makes her think of old-timeys with gaps in their teeth.

Everyone checked, we hadn't been calling her Ma.

Then we figured it was the day or the night, the horns in the street, or the boys playing ball. They knocked in her window, all of them did. I feel like those pilots, she said, great birds of prey, paying no mind, migrate through my house, my kitchen of all places. So then we were birds of prey, buzzards and big wing-flappers with no respect for the common watched pot.

We were left to fight with each other. My sister said I fed off people and spit them up again like owl pellets, block forms of mice came out of my mouth, she meant.

I keep dreaming that my cat has come back to life.

Tennessee bears sometimes still haunt my mother. She comes running out of the house, my brother sits on the grass while the bear stands by the tree. Nothing more ever happens, she says.

My cat is happy to see me. She is sorry she is dead, it was a mistake, but look, she says, I am back, I am not in the dirt, and there is meat on my bones where the skin hung that you always touched.

Looking back, it did not have to do with lily pads. A frog, four legs, two eyes, one mouth, Pilah-Palah, jumped into the water. Lily pads was something I had made up in my head. So, she said, you are becoming like me.

Canasta she played until her eyes became pissholes in the snow. Rudy and Rosemary took her glass from her hand and she did not even know. She lit her cigarettes to look awake, but the ashes grew long and fell off.

Racehorses behind the house she backed off with a broom, just to get to the garbage. Beauty or not, she said, those animals just want to kill or to run. She told the man, she would open the gate, let them run past the sights of downtown, if he did not keep them away from her pails.

One time we had to throw out a bed. The bed is not just a chair or a couch, she said, the bed smells like you do when you are dreaming and when you are lying with your hands behind your head, staring at cracks in the morning.

She listens to the TV, and says, the more they find dead in that plane crash, the more I like it, I think I should turn myself in.

Lumber covers her backyard, the landlord is making a shed. He put planks on the grave, she said, and you can't tell the dirt from the sawdust. She would lie on the trampoline, but she is afraid of getting off and not having the ground to put her feet on. Then she laughs. She says I can't even find Mercury, I am lost up or down.

LAWS
OF
N·A·T·U·R·E

One night we went into the pool and Don came up behind a tree and he blew a trumpet and scared Betty and I out of the pool and then he jumped on Jasper and came after us on Jasper. Betty and me screamed but Don kept on riding after us.

Betty and I ran out of breath at the cellar door. In the cellar were rattlesnakes that the kids liked to throw apples at. Some days the kids could get the rattlesnakes rattling so loud that you thought of locusts in the air and not of rattlesnakes down in the cellar.

Jasper didn't want to stand by the cellar. He kept on walking backwards and he kept on walking from side to side. I bet Don was holding Jasper's reins too tight. I was thinking that Jasper was probably wishing that he had been made to stop at any other place except the cellar.

Don blew his trumpet again.

It was not really Don's trumpet. It was one of the kids' trumpets and because I was used to hearing the kids blowing the trumpet and not Don blowing the trumpet all of the time, I thought that Don would be playing "Carnival of Venice" or something that the kids played on the trumpet all of the time and not just blowing on the trumpet the way a guard at the gates of a castle would.

Betty and I leaned on the cellar door catching our breaths. Because we did not have anything on, our tits hung down over the cellar door and I couldn't help but think that it seemed like I was offering the rattlesnakes down below the cellar door a tit at feeding time.

Don was still on top of Jasper, and he said that Betty and I being such close friends, that it would be a good thing. He said that now that we had all seen each other with our clothes off, the hard part was over. He said on all this land of Betty's that it would be like life before civilization. He said imagine the fish in the ocean. He said that there were laws of nature that we could not ignore.

I was glad it was still dark out. Even though Don saw me without my clothes on all the time, I did not want him to see me without my clothes on at just that particular time. I looked at Betty. She looked good. In the dark, you couldn't see all of the places on her skin that showed you she had children, like the rings on the insides of trees or the squares on turtles.

Don blew his trumpet again, and when he held it up, it looked like a toy and not the big trumpet that I was used to seeing the kids holding in their hands. I wished that he didn't have the trumpet. It made me think that in order for him to have gotten the trumpet he had to step on things in the kids' bedroom and he had to lift the kids' covers up that hung down from the sides of their beds so that he could look in all of the dark places for the trumpet while the kids slept.

Betty looked at me. They say that in the dark all that you can see of a person is the whites of their eyes and the whites of their teeth, but I saw Betty's hair. Betty's hair looked white in the moonlight even though Betty's hair was blond. I thought if Betty started running again, it would be of no use—Don, on Jasper, could find Betty anywhere on Betty's land with Betty's hair looking so white.

I saw Betty pull open the cellar door and run down the stone steps and close the door behind her. Because the rattling of the rattlesnakes got so loud after Betty opened the door, Jasper got spooked and ran down past the apple orchard and I heard Don yelling, "Whoa!" but I also heard Jasper still running.

In France I visited a man who had a house on the beach and he fell in love with me and he sent me back home in a car filled with roses. I could not see out of the windows because of the roses. My aunt Matilde, when she saw me get out of the car, said, "Marry him, marry him," and she pulled out the roses from inside the car.

I did not marry him.

My aunt Matilde sits on her bed with her pillows behind her and she tells me that I could have been a Countess. She tells me that I could have been the Queen of France. Then she puts her box on her lap and opens it and lifts up bracelets and rings and tells me what will someday be mine.

I want the malachite ring that she wears. It is not a precious stone. The malachite, I mean. It is maybe a semiprecious stone. I don't know. Aunt Matilde has let me try the ring on and it feels good on my finger. My fingers are shaped the same as my aunt Matilde's fingers are shaped and my aunt Matilde had the jeweler who made the malachite ring fit the ring to her finger as he made the ring and as he set the malachite stone in it. It is a ring, I tell Aunt Matilde, that the man who sent me home with the roses would not have thought to give to me as a wedding present. Aunt Maltilde says he would have given me the ocean instead.

We don't talk about Don, me and Aunt Matilde.

Jasper came back alone and I was surprised to see that he came back to the cellar. I was leaning over the door of the cellar telling Betty to come out. I was telling Betty that Don was gone. But she heard Jasper come back and she thought that both Don and me wanted her to come out so that we could both do to her what Don wanted to do with both of us earlier. I told her no. I told her Jasper was riderless. I told her Jasper might be the only friend we've got and that he left Don down by the road somewhere, alone, without his clothes on and a trumpet in his hand.

I said, "Come on, Betty, laugh," but she didn't.

Jasper licked my back and I think I screamed because at the time I did not know that it was Jasper. I thought it was Don. After I screamed, Betty opened the cellar door and I was glad to see her white hair but at the same time I wanted to cover her hair because I did not want Don to come after us again. But I had nothing to cover Betty's hair with. Our clothes were still out at the pool. I asked Betty if she was crazy to be standing knee-deep in rattlesnakes that already had it in for humans on this land in the first place because humans were always throwing things at rattlesnakes and getting them rattling so loud that no one near the cellar could think, or all they could think about was the sound of locusts in the air instead. Betty said, "I am not crazy, I am bit," and when I pulled her out, I could see by the moonlight that her foot was not its right size.

I got Betty on top of Jasper and then I got up on Jasper also and I started riding Betty into town, with her the whole time saying, "I am not a fish in the ocean."

. . .

My aunt Matilde told me that when she was young and she walked down the streets in the rain, men would lay down their coats on top of puddles that were in her way.

Aunt Matilde made me go to dinner with a man who was three times my age. She said if I married him I would be a Duchess. She said if I married him she would give me the malachite ring. I almost married him.

Riding in the dark, I hear Don blow his trumpet. He must have seen Betty's blond hair looking white, and he must have thought that we were going off to do it together—what he wanted us to do with him before, I mean. I put my heels into Jasper's sides but because I am barefoot, it must not feel like anything to Jasper so he does not move any faster than he would have if we were taking one of the kids on his back on a walk through the orchard.

My aunt Matilde, she tells me that it is a horror that I want a ring that is not made of rubies or of diamonds. She pulls out a ring that belonged to Marie Antoinette and it has a ruby in the middle and diamonds all around it. Aunt Matilde tells me that it is a ring like this that I should be wanting and I try Marie Antoinette's ring on, but I think to myself that the only kind of ring of Marie Antoinette's that I would want is the ring that Marie Antoinette was wearing when her head was chopped off.

When I turn around, I see that Betty's ankle is too big. Don is behind us. He is saying that it is his turn now. He is saying, "Think of life as the cavemen knew it." He is saying, "Think of the fish in the ocean." He is saying, "Think of all of the fish in the ocean."

I stop the horse.

I turn Jasper around to face Don and then I dig my heels into Jasper's sides so hard that I think to myself that I am imagining that my heels have spurs on them and that if I don't imagine that my heels have spurs on them that the horse will never move and never think to think that what I mean to do is kill Don.

I wear the malachite ring now. Aunt Matilde, when she died, told me to put Marie Antoinette's ring on her finger and then she asked me if that is what it would take to make me wear Marie Antoinette's ring, for her to have died wearing it.

Aunt Matilde, I mean.

I open the door and the kids are still sleeping. Don is on the floor of their room with the trumpet in his lap.

"I am lucky to be alive," he says to me. "You almost killed me on the horse," he says.

I tell him Betty was bit by a rattlesnake. I tell him Betty is swelling up.

He says, "The rattlesnakes and the kids," and then he says, "They understand the laws of nature."

ROUGH
S·E·A·S

Rebecca asks us why we call her Rebecca of Sunnybrook Farm. She does not ask why we also sometimes call her Breasty Rebecky. Then she says, "Who would know anyway why a name turns into lots of other names?"

Someone loses another chicken neck from their basket and says, "Darn, damn fool bugger." Rebecca says, "Damn fool bugger," too, and I think to myself all the damn fool bugger crabs she could catch with her breasties, more than we could catch with chicken necks.

I saw her once, swimming in the lake roped off into a square, and when she got to one end of the rope she did a swimmer's turn, the kind swimmers do off the walls of a pool. After she got out, I went in and looked for a wall, but you can't see too far down in the lake and you don't want to swim too far down, either. It gets too cold.

The cat is going to follow Riley that way, him on his bicycle, the cat running after him, behind the bicycle wheel, blinking its eyes every once in a while and running, following Riley. Riley rides away fast and the cat can't keep up with him and so the cat stops running and after it does, it just lies down in the road.

On the beach, I say, "Rebecca of Sunnybrook Farm," and I lay her down, her head near a burnt piece of wood from a bonfire. I hold on to the cheeks of her ass and I push into her so hard I think to myself that maybe I am pushing her across the beach and that we are headed for the water.

I buried our dog in our field and when, at night, I could not sleep, I went out to the field and lay down on the dirt that I had turned during the day. My feet stuck out onto the grass like I was sleeping on a bed that was too small for me and when I fell asleep I dreamt that the dog, in his hole under me, went back and forth and was digging with his front paws to make the hole bigger. When the dog got to the sides of the hole, he did turns like swimmer's turns, like the kind of turns she did.

I woke up hard. My dick pushing down in the dirt and it felt like I was poking a hole through the dirt because the dirt was soft and newly turned.

Walking hand in hand, Riley takes Rebecca walking down under the bridge. She's got a basket of chicken necks on her head, and she's walking like a girl in a good school with a book on her head. Riley turns and looks up at us and makes like he's going to pinch Rebecca's ass without her even knowing.

Rebecca cracks a bugger crab in half and someone says how would you like it if I lay you down and cracked you like that, away from your bone? But I see Rebecca pull the legs out and then suck on them.

. . .

I think to myself I am going to build a cabin on the field where I buried the dog.

After we push Rebecca down on the shells from the bugger crabs, her back bleeds.

When it is my turn, I call her Little Rabbit, not Breasty Rebecky like the others have done.

Sometimes you can catch them with just a rope tied around a chicken neck. Riley pulls one up slowly but when it falls away, he says, "Damn fool bugger, I could have saved him from years of rough seas."

Everyone is asking where she is. Riley and I go look for her on our bicycles. She is on the far side of the lake, lying on a beach towel, her face is down and her ass is in the air like a cat. Riley pokes at her arm with a stick and then he pokes at her ass with it. Then her breasts. Then Riley lifts up the stick up over his head and hits her hard on her back.

Sometimes I want to open the hole up and go back down under with my dog. Riley says I can't do it. Riley says to let the dog alone. Riley drops his line down on the pier and says from now on we have to catch buggers with our dicks and Riley takes off his pants and points his dick down to the sea.

TIDAL
A·I·R

So she could breathe she asked me to go up behind her and hold her ribs tight in my arms. I did it so many times that I began to think that as her ribs healed they must have healed with some of me inside them, like some of the bone from my own arms inside them, or maybe even some of my own breath inside them.

I never really was sure when it was that I could start to breathe again. I never knew when I would feel her take my hands and bring them down to her sides and away from her ribs. You see I always held my breath so that it would not escape, and so that maybe she could use it, so that maybe standing front to back with my mother my breath would do something like go from the inside of me to the inside of her.

Then sometimes I thought that my bone was too small for her and that my breath was too small for her also. I thought what she probably needed was a long big breath, a breath that had been outside for a while, collecting, a breath maybe from the air that had gone over lakes at night and come close to the sides of wooden barns and had taken off with it the warm smell from the sides of the barns where the day's sun had hit longest. I thought what she probably needed was some kind of breath that had been in a bear's den and touched the cool dirt on a bear's den ground. I thought a breath like that would be full of things to heal someone who was bigger than I was. This is what I had to think to myself, I had to think to myself that my breath has only been to the park on the corner, a park not even far away, a park close enough to walk to on the street barefoot if my mother is not looking.

Sometimes when I held her I felt around also. What I think I was feeling for was a hole in her side made from the handle. That is what broke her ribs. They broke on the handle that has the knob on it that you use to roll the window in the car up and down with. Set into the knob there was something silver, what it looked like was a cake decoration, a small silver bead, the kind she shook back and forth in the palm of her hand and waited for to fall from her hand through her fingers like it was sand she was shaking back and forth in the palm of her hand and not something that goes onto cake. I used to think that if I felt hard enough I could feel the cake decoration underneath her skin. But I never could feel it. I guess now that it never really was there in the first place, that it was just something I had made up in my head.

My arms used to grow tired from trying to meet across her ribs. I did not want her to heal with some of the bone from my tired arms. I did not know what to do. To make myself feel better, I used to imagine that I felt her hands take my own and bring them down to her sides, so that I knew that it was done, so that I knew that she could breathe by herself again. I became so good at imagining her hands taking my own that I think I can still imagine it. Not that I can see her doing it, or that I can see her hands, but that I remember the way it all felt to me. It was not that she did this and then that, it was like she did everything at once, and it was every-thing in the room at once. It was like the table in the room was not a table, but what it was, when I saw it, was a part of the way her hands felt to me when she brought them down to her sides. At that point, it wasn't even like she was my mother, it was like she was just her hands, her whole body was just her hands to me, and the way they felt when she touched my own. And I wasn't myself either, I was part of the whole thing also, like the table, I was something that I could step back and look at and say to myself, see, that is what it feels like when this person takes your hands and brings them down to her sides.

When I saw her fall from the step and run with her fall through the tall grass and tall flowers by the side of the house, I thought any moment now I am going to have to run up behind her and hold her again. After all these years, I am going to have to do it again.

In a way I wanted her to fall and to break her ribs again. And, for some reason, I thought I saw her wanting to fall also. As she was running with her fall, the tall grass and the tall flowers went up tall between her legs. I saw her push away at the tall grass and tall flowers, as if they were children as high as her hips who were wanting something from her, and she pushed away at them, as if she found a spot on the tops of their foreheads that she could push and make them go away because what she wanted most of all was to go back inside the house, to sit in a chair, and to just stay in one place. I thought that this is what gave her away to me. I thought that if I were falling, if anyone else were falling as they were running, the first thing that she would do would be to grab hold of some-thing to slow herself down, even if it was a handful of tall grass or tall flowers, she would reach for that or even thin air and not push it away. But I did not know why she would want to fall and break her ribs again. It made no sense, it was, I guess, something I wanted to see her want. I wanted to see her want to break her ribs again so that maybe she could give me another chance, so that maybe I could hold her ribs again and this time, the bone from my arms would be bigger and stronger, and my breath would have been to more places outside for a while, just collecting.

My head went through the windshield three times. I did not count it, it was what she told me. She was right there. I was sitting on her lap and next to us was the knob on the handle that you use to roll the car window up and down with. Now I try to remember what I was thinking right before it happened, but I can't. It was late in the day. I wonder if what I was thinking was that it was late in the day. I do not think so. What I think is that when you are little you do not think about things like late in the day. Maybe you think about lightness and darkness but not late in the day. Or shadows, when you are little I do not think you think about shadows. I do not even think that when you are little you think that shadows have to do with the sun. I can't say I remember thinking, when I was little, that shadows had to do with the sun. Maybe I just saw them and did not think about them.

I remember everything to the side of us that was on the same side as the handle. I remember the car window was open. What I think now is that that meant one of us, my mother or myself, had rolled it down, had taken hold of the knob on the handle right before it all happened. What I can't stop thinking is that when one of us touched it, right before it broke my mother's ribs, that one of us touched it and had no idea and did not even think to think that it could do such a thing. Did

not even think to imagine that the silver bead in the knob of
the handle could look like a cake decoration, a thing I used to
see her hold in the palm of her hand even. That scares me,
that makes me think that I should not touch or look at anything, and that maybe, back then, I would have been better
off blind.

By the roadside there was tall grass. I remember the tall
grass because now that I think about it, it reminds me of beach
grass because it blew in the wind. Really, all that I remember
seeing was the grass blowing in the wind. I am just thinking
now that the grass must have been like beach grass, and not
country grass, and that then, when I saw it, I did not even
think about the beach or what the grass looked like. All that
I saw was that it was blowing in the wind. That really is all
that I remember thinking about.

I could not see through the blood on my face. She said
she had thought I had been blinded by the glass. But I remember now, all that I knew then was that I could not see
and that it was dark. I did not think about being blind, that
was something she told me later that I should thank the heav-
ens for that I wasn't. I remember the darkness best of all. I
don't know why. It is still a picture in my head that I can
take out and see. Maybe I remember the darkness so well
because there was so much to hear in it. I heard my mother's
breath, skipping, I now know, because of the hole in her side,
and her breath was saying my name over and over again, so
many times that I began to think that it was the way her breath
had always sounded to me.

Sometimes I make myself imagine her as a child again,
because I don't think I remember what her breath sounded
like before it happened. Before it happened she must have had
a clear breath. The kind you get from standing up barefoot

on a swing and taking air in fast and not taking air in slow like you would if you were just sitting down in a swing. I imagine her as a child, standing up barefoot on a wood-seated swing and taking air in that comes off a bay or an ocean that her swing looks out to, and I try to imagine the breath she breathes out not sounding like my name being said over and over again, but I can't, because that feels like I am imagining someone else altogether.

When she fell off the step and ran through the tall grass and tall flowers she did not fall to the ground. There was no need for me to run to her and to hold her, so I just stayed where I was. Falling off the step and running with her fall did not break her ribs, not in the least bit, what it did was make her breathe harder. What happened was that my name was breathed so loud in the air that I thought that it must be drowning out things that had been in the country forever. I thought my name was drowning out a waterfall and drowning out the wind that blew through old husks of corn that were still on the stalk in the field and had never been picked. And, worst of all, I thought my name was drowning out my own breath. Then, I had to run inside the house, I had to sit down in a chair, in the quiet, and I had to listen for the sound of my own breath like my life depended upon it. I placed my hands on the warm wooden table and I closed my eyes that still had the sunlit picture of my mother pushing tall flowers and tall grass under them, and I listened. At first I could not hear anything, there was nothing at all. Then I imagined a wind, the kind that has been over lakes and against the sides of barns and in the dens of bears where the ground was cool. I listened harder, and still I did not think I could hear my own breath, so then I imagined the tall grass by the side of the road, blowing in the wind, and I imagined that it did not remind me of anything, that it did not remind me of beach grass because it blew in the wind and that I was sitting in her lap and there was her breath and my own. That is when I lifted my hands from the wooden table and walked outside.

WHERE
D·E·A·D
IS BEST

My brother said to me, "A man's got to be buried with his teeth in."

Out back, back where trees grew whose leaves looked like ferns, we walked over bricks and looked down at the ground. We looked for Jochen's teeth.

On the ground we saw things that used to be in our house. "Radio," my brother said. "Turn it on with your foot," he said.

I was the one who was close to it.

"Turn it on?" I said. "But it was once thrown out the window," I said.

"Plays old tunes, then," my brother said.

My brother leaned his hand against the trunk of a tree. "If Jochen's teeth are in these trees," he said, "then I don't know, are these trees just too thin to climb?"

We shook that tree and every tree hard, and waited under them as if shaking an apple tree and waiting for apples to fall.

When our necks got tired, we stopped shaking and looking up.

. . .

But we looked down and found a wallet on the ground. There was nothing in it. My brother held the wallet sideways in the air.

"This is the curve of some man's backside," he said. "Now find the man."

We put the wallet under a brick.

My brother said, "Like voodoo, the man walking the streets will feel a pain in his backside, making him stand up straight. Find a straight man," my brother said, "and we will have our man."

Then my brother fired his finger at me.

"Not here," I said. "I'm not going to play dead here."

"This is where dead is best," my brother said. "Fall down anywhere," he said, "Fall down, your back against the trunk of a tree and look like you're just sitting up, resting."

"You do it," I said.

I fired my finger at him.

He fell against a tree and slid his back down the tree's trunk. The leaves in the tree bounced up and down. My brother looked out somewhere. His eyes didn't move. I took a deep breath in.

I said, "Looky here," and I went and I kicked my brother's foot with my foot. "Looks familiar," I said. "Looks like something we had in the house once. No," I said, "too ugly to be in our house."

Then my brother grabbed my leg and pulled me down to the ground. I screamed. My brother fired his finger at me and said, "Dead, dead, a hundred times dead."

My brother said, "Jochen's teeth will come to us if we just remember the shape of his face."

. . .

We sifted dirt in our hands. "A dig site," my brother said. "An ancient city under us," he said. "And this, all this," he said. "Volcanic ash," and he took a piece of something from the ground and threw it up into the air.

I said, "Are you sure he said out back? Back out here?" My brother said, "Yes." He said, "Where else? Out front? Where someone could take them? No," he said, "when he opened the back window it was like he was opening a drawer and dropping something into it."

Back in our house, my brother said, "Tomorrow we try again." He swallowed lemonade from a glass jar. I thought I heard the jar hit his teeth when he got it up to his mouth.

"Boots like chapped hands," my brother said. "Cracked on the outside, that's what I remember best," he said.

We were lying in the dark in our beds.

"Boots?" I asked. "Boots is going to get us his teeth?"

"I don't know," my brother said. "Suck boots. Think face. Face gets teeth," my brother said.

I heard him turn under his sheet.

"Thinking?" he said.

"Yes, window," I said.

"Window? Why window?" my brother said.

"I don't know," I said. "Big and square—you know, the shape of his face."

"Keep that thought," my brother said, "and Jochen's teeth will come crawling to us on their hands and knees."

"*Cierra la ventana*," he said.

"What?" I said.

"I picked that up," he said. "On the train. A woman said it to her son and I heard her say it. *Siéntate*, she also said, *siéntate*. Sit down. Close the window," my brother said.

"Oh," I said.

"I'll think about the window also," my brother said. "In my head I'll call it Jochen's window." Then he said, "You hear that? Footsteps," he said, "Jochen's footsteps, walking in the house. Watching over us. Angel Jochen," my brother said.

"In the morning," he said, "first we go over to Jochen's house and walk around. We feel the walls. We see how they feel having him been living inside them for so long. Touch the floor," my brother said. "Touch the pots he touched. Then, shit," my brother said, "touch the pipe, too. Maybe even taste the pipe—and if the rope is still there," my brother said, "then who knows what."

The rope was still there.

We touched it.

There had been a loop, but it had been cut.

"To get him down," my brother said.

Then my brother made another loop in the rope and stood back and looked at the rope and looked at me and said he would need me, said with me in his arms we would be tall enough and I could feel the loop around my neck and tell him what it felt like to have a loop around your neck.

I said, "We haven't touched the pots yet or the walls yet. Aren't we going to touch the pots?" I said.

"We're lucky the rope is still here," my brother said, and came up behind me and lifted me up.

At first it was like bobbing for apples, except I was the apple and the rope was the one who was doing the bobbing. I didn't lift my hands to help the rope go over my head.

Instead, my brother tried to get me in front of the rope, as if he thought the rope would find my head if I was close enough to it. I wanted to scream, but I didn't want to scream in Jochen's house, a house, my brother said, that couldn't care less if it heard a little kid scream.

When my head was in the rope, my brother was saying, "Think teeth," and I thought teeth because I did not want to think about the way the rope scratched my neck or if there was some of Jochen's skin still on the rope. But I thought those things, anyway.

"Out back?" my brother asked. "Still out back?"

"Yes," I said. "I think so," I said.

"Okay," my brother said, and then let me get down.

My brother opened the door and went out back.

"You think window," he said to me, "then stay near the window. I'm going to the middle," he said. "I'm going to wait for his teeth to show their face."

I leaned against the wall of bricks, my head just under the window. I could see my brother sitting down and leaning against the tree that he had fallen against when I had shot my finger at him. He was looking the way you look at nothing or sometimes he looked like he was looking at me.

"*Siéntate,*" he said to me. "*Siéntate,* sit down," he said.

I sat down, I moved a brick out from underneath my backside.

"*Cierra la ventana,*" he said. "Close the window," he said. "Do it," he said. "Stand up and close the window," he said.

I stood up and put my foot in a hole in the wall made by a brick that had come loose and fallen out and I lifted myself up. I closed the window that had been above my head.

"There," my brother said. "Now come back down."

I got down on the ground again. I wiped my hands on my pants.

"Let's give up," I said. "There's no teeth out here," I said.

We walked through the trees. When we passed the brick that had the wallet that we had put under it, my brother pulled the wallet out and lifted it in the air again, to show me that the wallet had gotten straight. But it hadn't. The wallet was still curved.

"The way the man's backside is curved," my brother said, and then threw the wallet back down onto the ground.

When we came to the right tree, my brother made me put my hands together and make a step for him to step onto so that he could start to climb the tree.

I looked up, and because the sun was in my eyes I could not see my brother sitting in the top of the tree. But I heard him.

"Jochen," he said, "Angel Jochen."

THE
C·H·I·L·D·R·E·N
INSIDE THE
T·R·U·N·K

She tells me that when she wakes up in the morning her mother is sitting next to her in bed and watching her. She tells me that what is left of her mother's real hair sticks out from underneath her mother's wig. She says she herself is thinking of getting her hair cut like the wig her mother wears is cut.

She tells me that she read in a magazine that things are so dull in the outback of Australia that the men who drive the train that goes through the outback are glad when an animal is on the train track so that the men driving the train have something to do, something to watch when the animal is being killed. Then she says that the magazine said that the men liked to see any animal being killed, except, of course, the emu because the emu, the magazine said, left feathers for miles.

On the highway she reads a sign on a car's trunk and what the sign says is CAUTION: CHILDREN INSIDE, and she says, "Imagine that, there are children inside of that trunk."

She says, "I think that everything I touch is going to give me what my mother has." She says, "I imagine that my feet are two steaming irons that shoot steam out through their holes and don't let anything come up through their holes." She says, "I don't drink water in my house." She says, "I think maybe the water gave my mother what she has." She says, "At night, when I go to sleep, I imagine that the sound of the fan that is on in the attic is the sound of a waterfall."

In the car, she asks me, "Where are we?" and she says it so many times to me that it becomes a joke between us. I ask her, "Where are we?" and she says, "No," she says, "where *are* we?"

We pass by horses on farms, and I tell her to look, but she says, "Don't make me look," she says, "I am watching the road."

I see all of the dead animals on the road.

She calls them DORs, for Dead on Road.

We pass by a family who is sitting on a hill and watching the road and she says, "Remember the men who lined up on the deck and wore goggles and sat with their hands in their laps and watched the thing at Bikini?"

Her father is a lumberjack and at night he takes off his watch-band and lays it out flat on his lap and takes his knife and scrapes at the inside of his watchband with the blade of his knife and what he says he is doing is that he is scraping off the resin and the sweat from the inside of his watchband that collected there after a long day of cutting down trees. He dares us to smell his watchband. "It is a smell that is supposed to be worse than anything a human can smell of," he says. Then he says, "Except the smell of a dead human."

She smells it.

She says, "Never dare a Van Dyke," after she smells it.

She tells me that her name in Dutch means Juniper. I

know she means Jennifer, not Van Dyke. She tells me that
now she is drinking gin because gin is made out of her berries.
She tells me that when she sits with her mother when her
mother is sleeping, she drinks gin and doesn't have to be the
only one being watched in her sleep.

It is a good night for walking but we don't go walking anywhere. She shinnies up trees. She knows how to do it, she
says, because her father is a lumberjack and taught her how.
I stand beneath a tree she shinnies up and bark that she made
come loose from the tree with her foot falls down on my head.
Sitting up on a limb of a tree, she says, "It must be Thursday
because," she says, "I can see into my mother's room and my
mother is not wearing her wig."

She tells me that when her mother is in the bathroom her
father takes the handle off the bathroom door and her mother
tries to open the door but her mother can't. Her father says
to her mother, "What is the matter with you? Just open the
door."

She tells me that her father was once down by the stream
and he saw children by the side of the stream and he told the
children that he was a mountain man from Alaska, and the
children asked him what he ate in the mountains of Alaska,
and he told them anything, he told them he ate leaves and
then he lifted leaves up from the stream and he ate them but
what he was eating was a handful of jack-in-the-pulpit, and
jack-in-the-pulpit can cut his throat, he said, like thorns from
the stem of a rose would.

She tells me that she hears her mother and her father doing
it in the next room. She wonders if her mother does it with
her wig on or her wig off. She wonders if her mother does it
on Thursdays, is what she means, she says. She wonders if

her father imagines that it is a different woman when he does it. She tells me that she hears them tell each other that they love each other when they do it. She tells me that she wishes she knew how to take the door handle off their bedroom door when they do it.

We keep seeing the same kind of DORs on the road. She says, "Maybe it's the same one." She says, "Maybe it's coming back to life and laying itself down on the road again for us to see over and over again. Put your sunglasses on," she says. "Let's pretend we are wearing goggles and driving to the atoll."

Her father says that the woodpecker said that he did not know whether the tree was a birch or a beech but that it was the best thing he'd had his pecker in in a long time.

She tells me to watch out for the jokes her father tells, especially the joke about the woodpecker who did not know if the tree was a birch or a beech.

We get to Alta finally.

Alta is a ghost town.

She says her car can't make it up the hill to Alta, but she takes her car up there, anyway. Because the car bounces up and down on the road, when I look out the window I see the trees bouncing up and down. She says, "Maybe those trees bounce up and down all of the time and maybe it's not our car that makes the trees look like they are bouncing up and down."

There is nobody else on the road up to Alta.

There is no tumbleweed in Alta. There is a place that we think could have been a whorehouse. There are mattress springs still in some of the rooms. There is writing on the wall. We stand at a window without any glass in it.

"Did you know that Alta means high?" she says to me.

She walks around Alta looking for things that she can take back home. She finds pieces of dishes on the ground near back porches that lead to the kitchens of the houses.

"I am winded," she says. "The air in Alta is *muy alta*," she says.

We walk inside one of the houses. We go up one of the staircases and because there is no floor at the top of the stairs we walk across the beams, and she says, "This is not easy to do."

I see it first.

I don't know what it is. I don't know if it is an animal or a human. Then I see its claws, which are crossed and nailed to the wall. It has no hair, and I think to myself that it must have been skinned either before or after it was nailed to the wall. I go to see if it smells, but I can't smell it or anything else.

She sees me smelling and comes over. She pulls the nail that is in between the claws out. Because it has no hair, you can't believe it could ever look like it could stand on all fours and run out the door and back into the mountains. But it does look like it can stand up and run because it twitches. It stands there twitching, looking like it's ready to go somewhere and be with all of the other things that you have seen in your life that you didn't want to.

She tells me that she has seen a man with his foot on backwards and a man with no arms who danced. She tells me she has seen worse but she can't remember. She tells me she just changed her mind, that this one is the worst.

Upstairs, her mother calls her name, and she goes up with a bottle of gin to sit by her mother in bed and tell her mother about Alta. I sit in the living room with her father. He tells me he told his wife we went to Alaska, and not Alta, and that his wife was worried we didn't bring the right kind of clothes. Then he takes off his watchband and pulls out his knife and scrapes off the watchband with the blade of the knife.

S·T·O·R·I·E·S
IN ANOTHER
L·A·N·G·U·A·G·E

On a hillside in China my father told me that he would teach me to fly by the time I was nine and that he would teach me to drive by the time I was twelve. I never understood why my father wanted me to fly first before I learned how to drive. I guess it was because he liked flying best.

I never learned how to fly.

I learned how to drive by the time I was twelve, though.

I drove jeeps right before the war because there were so many jeeps around. My father said that the only things in the sky were the Jap planes these days, and he never brought up the idea of teaching me how to fly again.

Now we are living on a bad street, and Charlie invites up these people who he met off the street for drinks in our house. I'm sitting in the chair watching a woman pull out her tit from her shirt and start feeding her baby.

There, in that place, we ate fish heads. You could chew on the eyes of the fish. My father told us to think that it was like chewing on gum.

Our nanny went to them and asked them for milk for my sister. They said no. She asked again. They took a bayonet and cut a piece out of her leg off. Then the hole in her leg could be like a hole for my fist.

Now Charlie keeps walking to the window and looking down at the street. Because they are having fires in the trash cans down there, the light from the fires lights up Charlie's face all red. The woman with the baby at her tit isn't saying anything to anybody.

Before the Japs took my jeep, I drove it everywhere. I drove it up to the hill where my father liked to walk with me and I got out of the jeep and stepped back from it, just to see what a jeep looked like standing on a hill.

I took my friend down to the river in the jeep, and in the backseat was a sack of kittens her mother wanted us to dump in the river. But at the river we sold the kittens to people who wanted to eat them.

The dog is under the piano, growling at the black man. Charlie and I keep saying hold still to her, but she hates black people more than anything.

I am glad that the black man knows that the dog is watching him. I see a knife in the black man's belt like the kind everybody down in the street has these days.

I am wondering how I send my kids outside the house every day.

The baby's eyes are closed this whole time that it is sucking on the woman, and the woman is humming to herself, or to the baby. I can't tell for sure. It doesn't sound like a lullaby.

I made a brassiere for myself out of sheets. I got my period there also. They took us out every day, in the morning, to watch the squad do the lineup killing. They stuck a gun at the back of your neck so that you would watch. I liked the feeling of the gun on the back of my neck because it kept my mind off the pains in my stomach. It got so that I would look forward to the lineup killing in the morning on account of my stomach.

I am saying to myself thank God that my kids are asleep because two of the people that Charlie invited up are standing in my kitchen and they are kissing each other and licking each other's faces with their tongues very pointy.

I try to get Charlie's eye, but he is not looking at me. He is talking to a fat bearded man about our President.

I call the dog to my side because I am thinking that the black man is looking at me like he would like to lick my face like the two others are licking each other's. I pet the dog, but her ears are pulled back, and her head is tense, and it doesn't feel so nice to pet her. When the kids walk down the sidewalk with the dog, the dog never lets the kids get near the cars. She chases the kids toward the buildings like my kids were sheep and she was a sheep dog.

Before the war, my father was stationed at a training camp. He came home on leave one weekend and he told me that one night he went to bed and woke up in the middle of the night and saw a woman sitting in his chair, in his room, and then she took off her head and started brushing her hair. He swore to it that it was true and he swore to it that she was the most beautiful woman he ever saw.

The girl is sitting down on my kitchen floor and the guy is taking her shoes off and he is licking the girl's feet. Then he is pulling down a bottle of my soy sauce from the shelf and he is shaking it all over the girl's feet and then he is trying to lick it off her feet. The smell of the sauce is strong and Charlie looks up and sees what the two of them are doing and then he looks at me. I stand up and take the dog by the collar and walk into the kitchen with her. I take the cap from the sauce and screw it back onto the bottle, even though there is no sauce left in the bottle. I pull up hard on the dog's collar because she is bending her head down to the floor and trying to lick up the sauce that fell off the woman's feet, like this dog was a horse who stopped short in a gallop to bend down to eat grass by the side of a road.

Charlie comes into the kitchen and asks the two of them if they could take it easy in our kitchen. They ask if we have got a bedroom and Charlie tells them the whole city is one big bedroom and all they have to do is walk down the stairs and out of our place and onto the street if they want to lie down and fuck.

I wish he had taught me how to fly. I would have liked to have the memory of seeing our place from the sky before it got taken away. I guess if I need to imagine, I can imagine myself standing on top of the hill, looking down, and pretending I was looking from a plane.

I have stuck my fist in my nanny's hole in her leg. But lately, I guess, because of her age, and because of the wrinkles in her skin, the hole has gotten smaller, or seems to me smaller, so that now the hole doesn't take up all of my fist anymore.

The baby hasn't stopped sucking on the woman and I look at the tit and I think to myself that it looks like it's gotten smaller from having so much sucked out of it. The two of them in the kitchen take Charlie's advice and they go down the stairs, out of our place, and onto the street. The black man looks out the window, opens the window, and calls down to his friends. I am tired. I ask the woman how old her baby is. She looks at me and smiles and says she doesn't know, that she can't remember when she had it.

There were always sacks on the sides of the roads. They were bodies just killed that day, wrapped in cloth, and put out into the road for the trucks to come by and pick up. Because the bodies were fresh and did not smell yet, the little kids would sometimes sit on the bodies as if they were sitting on couches and they would play circle games in the dirt with sticks or with stones.

I took the elastic out of my mother's brassiere and I made a slingshot.

I became good with the slingshot.

I shot birds when I could and we ate them. I shot at rabbits. But you had to get rabbits right on the head if you wanted to kill them.

The black man is coming at me and then the dog goes for his neck.

I took the jeep to my cousin's and we liked lying on the jeep instead of lying next to her pool and getting the sun.

The black man is running down the stairs. The dog is holding onto his neck with her teeth and her legs are hanging in the air, looking like she will never let go.

There is blood all over.

The woman with the baby is looking down at the blood and telling me that now she remembers he is two months old.

I go to the top of the stairs and the black man and my dog are gone. There is blood on the handrail in the shape of the black man's hand, as if the black man remembered to hold on to the handrail while he ran down the stairs so that he would not fall. I picture that the dog must have been holding on to the black man's neck, her feet in the air, looking like the fur of a fox whose tail and whose feet hang down the back of some person's neck.

Sometimes I dream of going back, not to the place, but to my house. I wonder if the house is still there and if the hill is still there.

Sitting in my jeep, I used to look up at the Jap planes and think that they were our planes and that one of the pilots was my father and that he was waving down to me as I had my legs swung over the steering wheel of my jeep and my girl-friends are all sitting beside me, playing the radio and chewing on gum.

We don't call the police. The fat man with the beard and the woman with the tit and the baby leave. The woman, as she goes down the stairs, holds on to the handrail with one hand and holds on to the baby with the other hand. She puts her hand right onto the spot on the handrail with the blood on it from the black man.

Back in the house, it still smells to me like the sauce.

When I tell my children that the guerrillas saved us, they say they can't help but think of gorillas in a jungle coming through the barbed wire at the place and picking us up in their hairy arms and carrying us away.

. . .

I stay up and wait for the dog. When she comes in, she is smiling a dog's smile and she puts her head on my leg. When I pet her I can't feel any blood in her fur. But how could she have licked the blood off her own head?

Years afterwards, my father learned the American song *I want to be an Airborne Ranger, I want to live the life of danger*.

At night, he sang that song to my firstborn. He sang it like it was a lullaby—only he sang it in Chinese.

A
G·O·O·D
FATHER

Long ago I was taken by elephant to stand before the Sphinx at sunset.

My father took me up to the Sphinx and then my father covered my hand with his hand and we touched the stone.

He is standing on the porch, ready to go out with the dogs.

I want to be his pants because they are straight and tall and when he walks the wind cuts along the sides of his front seams as if each leg of his were a fin and the air were deep water.

This day I get to go out with him and the dogs. He takes my hand and I am reminded of fish alongside whales swimming close to them. He calls me minnow now anyway.

I am no taller than the place where he bends his legs.

I walk on his shadow as we walk and because it has not rained in days, when we walk we are putting our feet down always in circles of dirt that hang close to the ground, the way I think when snow falls, and when it sometimes falls slowly, it falls so slowly that it does not look like it is coming down or going up but it looks like it is just hanging there and is waiting for someone to tell it to fall.

The two big dogs he has trained so well that they know, without his telling them, to stand at his sides so when he walks down the road they are like his arms, moving when he moves.

Those two dogs. My father puts meat on the ends of their noses and then my father makes them stand that way for so long I get to see dogs eyes' water. Then my father does something I do not even see but only the dogs see and they, like snapping at flies, flip up the meat in the air on the ends of their noses and eat the meat finally. Then my father lets the dogs leave his sides and they run down the path that circles the marsh.

My father's arm is around me and his other arm is pointing to birds. He is telling me what the names of the birds are. When he points it looks as though the birds stand still in the trees so that they can be named by my father.

The dogs come running back and then run away again and then once again they run back. My father says they have something to show us. When we come across it, my father still has his arm around me and I am ready for him to tell me what the name of it is. Already the dogs have pulled at the legs and chewed the skin and, like puppies, they have bitten the toes of the boy who hangs in the tree. I can see out the side of my eye that my father's pants have fallen and he with them and I am thinking only about how to get my father to stand back up so that the wind can keep going around the sides of the seams of his pants and we can cut through the air on the path that circles the marsh as we go. Then my father takes me in his lap and turns me toward him so that I cannot see the boy in the tree and now there is only my father to think about and the dogs barking so loud that I can hear them barking up through my father's heart and I dream while I am awake that my father is turning into a dog.

We are that way forever.

So long that I begin to think that by now the dogs must be done eating the boy and that when I turn around there will just be the tree, and a bird, and my father pointing, telling me the name of the bird.

When finally my father stands, he lays me facedown on the ground and tells me to wait and tells me not to turn around and that if I do turn around then something will happen, something where I might never see him again.

The ground is like my father.

Up from it I can still hear the dogs barking and up from it I know that it is something that is all over, even under the water of the marsh it is there and I can find it easily, the way I can find my father.

I hear my father cutting. He is cutting the rope.

I know it is the rope but I begin to think to myself that he is cutting the dogs because he is mad at the dogs, but then I know one of the dogs has just come over to sit by me, the way my father has sent them to my side when I have had to take walks alone, so one dog comes over and sits by me and I hear my father calling him a good boy.

I am still lying facedown on the ground, but then I start thinking that I want to turn around to see if my father is still wearing his pants because I begin to think he has taken his pants off to cover the face of the boy and I am scared that my father will be standing bare-legged when I turn around and we will never get back because there will be nothing to cut the wind as we walk.

I am just about to turn around and save my father's pants

when I hear my father tell me to think good things and then he calls me minnow and tells me a story while I hear him working and cutting and the leaves in the trees shaking as if a wind were circling in them and caught there the way leaves on the ground get caught in the wind and circle without stopping and stay in one place like slow-falling snow.

Once upon a time we rode elephants to see the Sphinx at sunset and when we got to the Sphinx I took your hand and we walked together to the Sphinx and we touched the stone of the Sphinx and we felt that what was coming up through the stone of the Sphinx was cool and when we left the Sphinx and rode back on our elephants we could still feel the cool stone of the Sphinx on our hands and even years later, after I died, you would still sometimes feel the coolness in your hand and you would know I had been your father.

Like two sled dogs, my father has strung the boy to the dogs with the legs of his pants and we walk back. The boy going slowly, so slowly that he is not really going anywhere, and the dogs not moving, and my father just holding me, and I am afraid it will be this way forever.

THE
K·I·L·L·E·R

Buffalo Bill, *what did you kill?* That was the song that my brother used to sing to me about buffaloes. He sang it to me when he put me to bed. This is what my brother did when he put me to bed—he looked at me and he sang and he made the blankets tight around me. I remember I thought to myself that my brother thought that Buffalo Bill was me, that as my brother looked at me and sang and made the blankets tight around me, that he was asking me, his sister, what did I kill.

A NOTE ON THE TYPE

This book was set in a digitized version of Janson. The Linotype cutting was made direct from type cast from matrices long thought to have been made by the Dutchman Anton Janson, who was a practicing type founder in Leipzig during the years 1668–1687. However, it has been conclusively demonstrated that these types are actually the work of Nicholas Kis (1650–1702), a Hungarian, who most probably learned his trade from the master Dutch type founder Dirk Voskens. The type is an excellent example of the influential and sturdy Dutch types that prevailed in England up to the time William Caslon developed his own incomparable designs from them.

Composed by Crane Typesetting Service, Inc.,
Barnstable, Massachusetts

Printed and bound by The Haddon Craftsmen, Inc.,
Scranton, Pennsylvania

Designed by Tasha Hall